Wasteland

by

Fox Robinson

Table of Contents

1 – A Willing Pawn -pg. 3

2 – Painful Memories - pg. 41

3 – The Madam – pg. 50

4 – A Magical Place – pg. 61

5 – A Plan Forms – pg. 102

6 – Revenge is at Hand – pg. 143

7 – Taken – pg. 164

8 – The Orgy Room – pg. 169

9 – Victory – pg. 203

Wasteland

Chapter 1

A Willing Pawn

The setting sun bathes the landscape in an eerie red glow. There is a harsh beauty in this broken light. After the fall, the world became a wasteland and left little to be admired - these pretty sunsets paid for at such a high cost. Taking in this broken world around me. Watching as the never-ending winds blow the dusty soil almost constantly into the sky. Leaving a permanent state of dusk with the darkness of night, bringing the only reprieve from the dismal scenery that unfolds endlessly before my eyes.

The sun casts a dark shadow across the door of the broken house in front of me, as the hot air blows and swirls around me, rustling my skirt, revealing the cache of weapons I keep hidden underneath it. Another dark reminder of the times lay strewn before me. Chaos and destruction reign here.

As I step over the twisted remains and approach the door, the familiar tinge of excitement starts to creep through my body. His motorcycle is here—that explains the carnage. What was so important that all these men were willing to die to protect it? Judging from the contorted looks and broken angles the lifeless bodies are left heaped in, they did not go quietly. My excitement and curiosity brims at the melee I might find waiting for me on the other side of that door.

The rusty clasp easily gives way with a kick from my boot. I am obviously not the first to enter without knocking. The door swings open. Removing my goggles, I step inside and let my eyes adjust to the feeble light in the dingy room.

My attention is immediately drawn to the figure standing by the fireplace. His tall muscular frame outlined by the firelight, casting a broad ominous shadow that seems to reflect the darkness of his soul. As my eyes trace the bristling muscles of his body, I can make out the scars on his face, arms, and chest. Trophies in this world where words mean nothing, and power is held in the hands of the most ruthless among us. I know his scars; I have watched him work. I know he is not the type to flinch at pain, or shy away from an opportunity to inflict it. I have watched as he took blows that would kill any normal man, laugh as his victims pleaded for mercy just moments before he ended their miserable existence. I have seen his body go from unmarked and pure, to this chiseled and battle-hardened warrior. Each scar telling a more horrifying tale than the last, a tale of either a brutal battle or of an overzealous, and often the case, treasonous lover. His taught shoulders and muscular arms seem to be cut from stone. Swollen biceps leading to thick forearms and giant hands with fingers like tree branches. His legs like tree trunks, thick and powerful are wrapped tight in leather, stained with the blood of his vanquished foes. His heavy boots marked by the harshness of surviving in this land, but more recently from the teeth of those whom he chose to stomp out the life of outside instead of on wasting a bullet. His brutality often sickens me. I know where the pain comes from that drives him, I know why he is here, and why all these people died such horrible deaths. We share a mutual goal but use very different tactics to achieve it.

He catches me staring. My eyes lock with his, they are almost glowing in the dark.

It would appear that I have arrived just in time. Without just a simple nod to acknowledge my arrival he moves swiftly to the door at the far end of the room. It is well built. Obviously installed as a last line of defense to keep anyone out who managed to get past the guards outside. We have encountered these doors before, and all to aware that blasting through it will only end up destroying the prize on the other side.

"My lady, if you wouldn't mind" He request with a sarcastic bow. Moving to the side to allow me to work with what little light there is.

I produce my pick kit from my satchel and begin working on the three locks on the door. For those of us not blessed with the power of brute force skills like picking locks and slight of hand often become our most powerful weapons out here.

I make short work of the three locks and with a final "click" the door swings open. My companion is impressed.

"My god women, I swear you get faster at that every time. It almost makes me wonder why they even bother locking the damn things at all knowing you're out here."

I give him a quick smile as I tuck my tools back into my bag and pull out my revolver. As we step into the dark hall lights are triggered and a long staircase is revealed. We begin down it. Careful not to set off any lingering booby traps.

The bottom of the stairs opens into a well-lit room. Large displays with numbers meaningless to me cover the wall. In the center of the room is a table. On it, our prize.

She looks to be 18 or 19. Pale skin untouched by daylight and long flowing red hair, cut to a length that looks to be about the middle of her back. The cumbersome mask over her face is connected to wires running back to the walls along with several other wires taped and strapped to her body. Her body is only lightly covered with a sheet, most of which has fallen away as she moans and writhes in front of us.

She is one of the Governors toys. Locked away down here until he decides he has a use for her. To keep her docile, she is connected to these machines that trick her mind into thinking she is in some sort of fantasy while the cords on her body drain her energy, making her too weak to run should she wake up.

My lover moves next to her, examining her.

"Well I don't know what she is dreaming about, but it must be good!"

The girl's hands explore and squeeze her body and her moans get louder as her fingers slip inside her wet garden.

"It almost seems cruel to wake her before she's finished." I think to myself. Time however is not on

our side. She could be like this for days and we only have a few hours before more guards show up.

"Alright, pull the switch" I command.

He complies and as the numbers go dark on the wall. I remove the mask and wires from her body. The moaning stops and as she opens her eyes terror falls across her face.

"Who are you? What is going on?" She cries, falling from the table and clamoring to the corner of the room. Trying desperately to cover herself with the sheet. "Oh god, have you come to take me to him? I'm not ready. Please I'm not ready!"

Her fear is understandable. No one that goes to see the Governor ever seems to come back.

"No." I reply. Were here to help, were here to set you free.

Still cowering in the corner, she looks around at the both of us. I can tell she isn't sure she believes me, but she wants to.

"Come with me. I will show you"

I extend my hand and help her to her feet. With her sheet still wrapped around her she cautiously follows me up the stairs. As we enter the empty room, she looks around slowly. Fearful that the men who held her here will appear at any minuet and force her back downstairs, or worse, take her away to him.

"They can't hurt you anymore." I say. Pointing out the window at the bodies still lying where they fell in the dirt.

A smile crosses her face briefly before she turns and embraces me. Apparently, I have earned her trust. Her lips are suddenly pressed to mine. Before I can reach her hands pull my face to hers, letting the sheet drop away. Instinctively I kiss her back. Our lips part and our tongues meet. The passionate kiss is arousing to say the least. Her amorous advances come as no surprise. So many of those we have saved have such a heightened libido they practically throw themselves at us. I have learned it is best to go with it. So many years spent forced into thinking your value is in your flesh turning them away tends to break something in their minds turning them into helpless, unpredictable beast.

"I have been stuck in that stupid hole almost my whole life with only that stupid visor as a link to any other human interaction." She walks to the center of the room, her naked body bathed in the firelight. "Now I'm free and I intend to thank you, both of you…" Her smile turns mischievous as she pulls us both toward her. "I don't have any possessions, I hope my body will be enough?"

As I admire her taught frame and perfect tits, I almost feel guilty wanting to take advantage of this poor girl. But this is Wasteland, moral conundrums aside, flesh is a currency and pleasure a commodity. Most importantly everyone in Wasteland is taught from day one, don't offer anything up in trade you aren't to give.

She can see I'm hesitant. Her hand runs up my leg and under my skirt brushing my now soaking panties.

"I wouldn't offer if I didn't want you, and I really really want you." She whispers into my ear. "Both of you, I want you to do whatever you want to me. I want to feel real bodies against mine for the first time!"

"Who can argue with that?"

I allow myself the pleasure of running my finger across her face. Her delicate cheekbones and pale smooth skin excite me as I let my nails scratch the skin on her long thin neck before I wrap my hands around it and look her dead in the eyes. Her deep green eyes are full of excitement. Her slender neck and frail frame entice me to grab her long hair forcefully as she drops to her knees. I am drawn to her ample breast tight stomach, narrow hips and her long slender legs and tiny feet. As her taught body trembles, I continue my inspection of her minimal but well-formed body. Her pale skin is clean and free from any blemishes giving away her plight. This girl is a prisoner, locked away, like a trophy for some demented master she has never met. She only knows she is his property and one day he will collect her to use as he pleases. She was imprisoned here, never to see the harsh world around her in order to keep her pure until he was ready for her. Her only crime was her immense beauty, and soon to be destroyed innocence.

My shadowy companion speaks. "It would be rude to turn down such a gracious offer."

As I inspect our prize more closely, I notice the tattoo on her hand. About one inch by one inch square it is really just a series of dots and circles. Meaningless to us but hidden in the unique pattern is all the information the Governor wants about her. I know this tattoo, I know this symbol. I have spent my life destroying everything I could find that has been marked with his wretched insignia even though I too have been branded by him, as has the other liberator of this fragile doll before me. I rub my fingers across it, secretly hoping it will rub off and we can spare this creature the horrid future that awaits her in this cruel world. A seemingly endless battle to regain what little dignity can be found in this place. Constantly on the run, never able to truly trust anyone. She has been rescued from a life of physical servitude to life of violence and danger with just enough pleasure thrown in to keep us all from just giving up. Not even a smudge and judging by how much it's faded it looks as though she was marked before her first birthday. Even if my companion is able to get her to the resistance, with that mark she will forever have to look over her shoulder for the Governors men.

"Looks like the old governor had this one picked out for himself. Should we ruin her for him?" I ask.

"It wouldn't do much for our reputation if we didn't," he replies, effortlessly pulling her to her feet effortlessly causing an excited gasp of frightened protest.

Unable to resist my primal desires any longer, I pull her face to mine once again. Her soft lips igniting the fire inside me.

"I like it rough by the way" she says coyly. Pulling away from my embrace as if to tease me to chase after her.

 I marvel at her spirit—even while it is so clear that her future is completely in our hands, she toys with us, controlling the room.

He yanks her hair back hard, making her cry out in pain as her body goes tense. I find myself getting aroused at this poor naked creature brought to submission so ruthlessly by this unfeeling man. Like breaking the spirit of a wild dog and bringing it to heel, suddenly eager to do its new master's bidding. She moans seductively, seemingly excitedly anticipating what is to come. She has no idea what is in store for her yet as she stands next to him in quiet obedience. Instinctively she tries to cover herself. Unsure of her role in this new fantasy she willingly has chosen to play a part in. The damsel in distress, captured by two beast who want to ravish her. She is no stranger to playing the victim but now she uses her perceived innocence to drive us wild. Her thin arms do little to hide her voluptuous bosom, her tiny hands unable to cover the deep red pubes decorating her barely blossomed flower. The desire to ravish her delicate naked body is consuming me. I feel the burning inside of unapologetic lust and wanton desire. I must have her now and I must have them both!

I know he will soon take us. Me willingly, her forcefully. I have seen this play out dozens of times, and each time I am more excited than the last. I strip away my weapons, giving him a clear sign that I am ready to have him inside me. I can feel my wetness with every step I take toward them. I can see his bulge growing as his excitement mounts. I know how much he wants me. He has always found our little dance to be erotic and I know he will not be satisfied until he completely fills us both.

He releases her to stand naked, staring at us as we embrace. Our passion meant to stir in her all of her deepest desires. I can feel her eyes on my body. Her gaze traces every inch, every curve of my form, her lust for me just arouses me more. He pulls me in for a passionate and long overdue kiss. My senses are overwhelmed by his touch, the feel of his body strong and solid against mine, even his scent. Like the earth itself. His powerful grip keeps me tight to him. As our lips part and I feel his tongue enter my mouth, I relish the feeling of being so powerless in the arms of such a dangerous man. His taste is always surprisingly sweet and somehow cool. It reminds me of mint and clean water. Impossibly delicious and soft for a man who has such a rugged exterior. I feel myself getting lost in the kiss, his lips taking me away from this god forsaken place, almost like floating.

His muscular arms enveloping my body, pulling me tighter to him, I pull his face to mine and our lips lock together again. It feels like it's been so long! I missed the taste of him, the feel of his body against mine, even the smell of his sweat. Every passionate breath I take in his arms brings back memories of ecstasy-filled encounters and forbidden pleasures. Tonight, would prove to be the best so far.

His hands begin to explore my body. Even over my clothes his touch arouses me. I long to feel his fingers on my bare skin but relish the excitement of his wandering grasp as it ignites my flame and stokes my desire emanating from everywhere he touches. His hands run down my back, causing me to arch, allowing my head to fall away from him. His mouth finds my neck and his teeth bite the skin. I moan as the sensation of his teeth on my bare flesh gives me goosebumps up and down my body. His soft lips dryly kissing as he continues to bite and nibble away at my exposed flesh, just enough pressure to drive me wild, seemingly harder with each bite. I am enthralled in the moment. I never want him to stop! His hands reach my waist and he circles around behind me. Pulling me tight to him, pushing my head forward to give his ravenous lips access to the nape of my neck. I close my eyes to relish the moment, get lost in the feeling of him behind me, his enormous bulge pressed into my backside.

I open my eyes to notice the naked standing before me. Her attempts to cover herself seem to be as much a show for us as an instinctual reaction for her. We appear to be arousing her—a feeling she has not had the pleasure of sharing with others up until now.

As he embraces me from behind, we turn to face our new toy. Her body is trembling, and her eyes are glued to the floor. Too scared at what looking up at us might mean for her! I find myself disturbed at her transformation. So easily she went from a wild spirit to this broken creature standing helplessly in front of me. She seems weak, scared, just another victim of this ruthless land. Just another girl we have to save to keep her out of the governor's hands. As I watch her though, she finds her courage, and her eyes meet mine. I'm impressed, all of the others tried only to please us when we released them. She is just standing there, suddenly proud and tall. Naked in front of us as though she has no fear of what we might do to her body, only that we might stop before she is satisfied. I am again aroused by her spirit, feeling only the slightest tinge of remorse at excepting payment in flesh. I justify it in my mind.

"After all it would be a shame if we had not saved her and let the Governor rob the world of such a marvelous specimen".

The tinge quickly fades, and the lustful desire returns as his strong hands begin pulling away my garments.

He undresses me. Working the straps and buckles on my jacket first, pulling it off to reveal my corset and shoulder armor. The tops of my breast bare to the world. I pull his head down hard against me as his hands travel over my body and loosen the straps of my corset. I stare intently at the girl. She is trying to play her role as the sub and not to meet my gaze, but her baser desires are overcoming her. As she watches him peel away the layers of my clothing, I catch her starting to run her hands across her breasts. She gently brushes her fingertips against her hard nipples and bites her lower lip. I reach out and forcefully lift her chin. There can be no doubt I am in control. She's forced to meet my gaze she instinctively tries to shy away but I hold her tightly by the jaw. She lets out a pleasing whimper.

He strips away the last of my clothes leaving me standing in nothing but my boots and choker. He steps back to admire his work. I know how much he likes watching the naked female form and I plan to drive him wild with it tonight. Still grasping her chin, I pull her body to me. Our breasts touching, her soft skin feels electric against mine. I have always loved the soft touch of another woman and I plan to get my fill tonight. I hold her face to mine. Our lips meet—she kisses me gently at first, then hungrily presses her soft lips against mine. I thrust my tongue into her mouth, and she moans as she lustfully reciprocates. I work my tongue around hers. To my delight I feel the gentle touch of her small hands on my breasts. I break away from her to watch as her fingers cross my nipples. Teasing them to erection and exciting me further.

"I've never seen another woman in the real life before," she squeaks out in a tiny and feeble but oddly arousing voice.

I take a slightly demented pleasure in this poor girl's complete lack of awareness of her situation. Even with her lifetime of training in the arts of pleasure and seduction the virtual learning programs that have been pumped into her brain by the Governors mind control device can't prepare her for what we are about to do to her. I know I must be careful not to shatter whatever trust or bond she feels we have built by both being female at the mercy of the same man. After all, I am here by choice. She has never been allowed to choose anything in her life. I feel an evil grin growing across my face. It's time to show this little bitch what she's been missing out on living down in that hole.

I grab her by the pubes, pulling hard and whisper into her ear loud enough for him to hear. "Well then, tonight is going to have a lot of firsts for you. And if you're a good girl I will let him make you cum. Now on your knees, bitch."

She drops to her knees, suddenly fully realizing her role in this little fantasy. She is my sub and for tonight she is at my mercy. A nervous and excited look spreads across her face. The invigorating rush of having this kind of power over another person races through me, making my whole body tingle.

He moves in next to us, standing close, not wanting to miss a moment of the excitement. I direct her to uncage the bulge in his pants. He moans with approval as his hands continue to explore my body. Rough hands, strong and coarse from a lifetime of devious acts. Gripping and pulling my body against his with no effort. His solid chest a wall against which he slams my back. His cock throbbing and hard pressed against my bare ass.

"Tonight, you are going to learn to suck cock, get fingered, have your pussy eaten, gapped, stretched, and fucked in every hole. But first," I grab her hair as I prop my leg on a chair "you are going to learn to eat pussy."

Sheepishly, she nods her head.

"I think this bitch is starting to figure it out." He chimes in.

I lean over and kiss him grabbing his cock with my free hand. I feel the girth of it fill my palm. I can barely get my fingers around it. Breaking the kiss, I turn my attention back to her and with both hands on her head I give her my instruction.

"Make me cum, you slut."

I pull her head into my pussy and feel her lips part as the tip of her tongue begins to slowly trace the edges of my waiting lips. Slowly, along the length of each petal of my labia. Then barely piercing inside me as she bares the width of her tongue up to my clit. Gently at first, she teases it then aggressively slips it back down inside me. Soaking wet I can't stop moaning her tongue impossibly deep in me then seamlessly slipping back to my clit.

I pull her head harder against me. "More, I want more!" I mutter between cries. Without missing a beat, she runs her fingers up along my pussy lips pressing in, forcing my clit out for her ravenous consumption. I feel her inside me again, her tongue, followed by two fingers. She can feel me and my soaking pussy quiver as her tongue is again at my clit. Excitedly she beings thrusting her fingers in and out of me, hungrily lapping the juices dripping off my box and sucking my clit. Barely stopping to catch her breath.

He is supporting me from behind, strong hands squeezing my breasts, teasing my nipples, as he bites and kisses my neck and shoulders. I release her head, but she only intensifies her efforts to satisfy my body. Her tongue seems to be everywhere at once—moving in all directions, pressing and sucking my clit from all sides, moving with my now gyrating hips, pressure for just long enough, then away to just tease with the tip of her tongue or completely taking me in her mouth.

Almost as much for support as pleasure I reach back and grab his massive rod. Rocking my hips violently, I can tell I'm driving him crazy. He moans as I wipe the pre-cum from his dick. I pull her head back and shove the wet fingers into her mouth. The salty taste surprises her, but she eagerly licks my fingers clean, then hungrily dives back down to my waiting pussy. I marvel at the site of her face dripping with my wetness as she looks up at me for approval, her eyes aglow with the excitement of the moment. I know the look of pleasure is written across my face by the way she smiles at me just before sucking my clit in past those tight little lips making me buck wildly. Overwhelmed by the sensation.

"I want your cock inside me!" I whisper in his ear biting his neck as I guide him between my legs.

"Put him inside me!" I order her.

She grabs the shaft and presses the tip into me. Moaning louder I scream "Oh God, yes, put him in me now! Please, please, I need it."

She pauses and lets him push through her hand, burying his massive dick deep inside me. She watches the first couple of strokes of this massive member splitting me in two, then feverishly laps at his cock and my pussy, trying desperately to please us both. I moan, a primal desperate sound that erupts from my lips as the pleasure of his cock filling me and her tongue teasing my clit crashes through my body! Wave after wave ripples through me. To my delight the two of them have found a rhythm and I am just a helpless ragdoll soaking up the movement of their bodies as each pounding thrust is followed by the increasingly vigorous licking and sucking of my clit. The feeling of being fully stretched and completely full has me thinking that I can't reach any higher state of ecstasy when I feel her finger slip inside me rubbing his cock and pushing me over the edge.

I cry out in ecstasy, begging them for more. They enthusiastically oblige me, continuing their quest to bring me to orgasm. I can feel it growing in my fingers and toes as his rhythm increases, it moves across my chest as he squeezes my breasts harder and then deep inside, the explosion.

"I'm cumming. Oh God, I'm cumming!" I yell as I find myself thrusting hard against his cock while forcing her face tight against my quivering mound and soaking lips.

He holds his cock deep in me while each contraction tightens around it and then slowly ebbs. My entire body is consumed by the sensation. My muscles ache as the feeling travels from every extremity back to the center of my body, finally releasing me from lusts grasp! Shaking from adrenaline and pleasure, I release her, letting her drop to the floor, enjoying the strong embrace of his arms around me as my body slowly quiets. After a few moments, I pry his arms away and dismount from his still rock-hard member. Slowly, so I can enjoy every inch as it slides out of me. As much as I would have loved to stay in his arms, lingering and enjoying the rush of this moment, our time is short, and the wasteland is no place for the sentimental. I have no intention of getting distracted from our purpose here. I quickly turn my attention to our willing host.

"That was quite a show you put on just now. You might do all right out here after all," I remark to her.

She smiles weakly. It's obvious she put a lot of effort into her performance. Fortunately, her night is just beginning. I turn to him, stroking his shaft slowly from tip to balls. It's still glistening with my juices. Kissing him gently on the lips, I smile coyly. He returns my smile and our attention is returned to the naked body in front of us. Now back on her knees, waiting obediently for her next instruction, her long hair matted with sweat as small beads of moisture drip down her naked back. Her submissive posture again awakens my desire to violate every orifice in her body. I push her down to her hands and knees with my boot heel, letting it press into her shoulder until she lets out a cry of pain. The hard floor causes her to shift uncomfortably as the old wood digs into her skin.

"I believe that makes it my turn," he pipes in. Licking his lips and giving my ass a firm squeeze.

I kneel beside her, pulling her hair back so her face is directly in front of his throbbing cock. With my free hand, I smack her ass as hard as I can. She cries out loudly—the sting in my hand is almost as exhilarating as the pleasure I get from her cries of pain and I continue to smack her cheeks until both are bright pink, my handprints clearly outlined on her pale skin. I like her pitiful squeaks and jam my thumb deep into her asshole. The shock of the sudden penetration, almost as overwhelming as the surprising pleasure from my intrusion into her most forbidden orifice, causes her to scream loudly and beg me not to stop. Her cries encourage me more. I thrust my thumb as deep into her as I can manage, causing her to lift her whole body. I yank her hair, bringing her back down hard against my probing hand. I let my free fingers slip into her tight little pussy. The confused and contorted look on her face shows her loss at understanding the link between pleasure and pain. Her pussy is sopping wet from the excitement of being penetrated, but her body shakes from the pain I am causing her. Her cries become moans as her mind goes blank and she gives in to the conflicting sensations tearing her sanity apart. Just as she begins to collapse, I release her, thrusting her head towards his cock.

"Clean him up slut," I bark at her. "And if I find one drop of my pussy juice left on him, I will shove my fist so far up your asshole you'll die choking on my fingernails."

I see the excitement return in her eyes, only this time it's quickly replaced by hunger. I have broken her down even further now. Whatever qualms she may have had about getting violated were quickly dissipating, and the lust she has felt for so long is clearly taking over. Her mind no longer tries to make sense of the situation, just her desperate desire to please us and be pleased by us, coupled with an uncontrollable physical desire she never knew she had. Her lust for our abuse has turned to a need she can only understand as an insatiable desire. I marvel at how quickly we have turned her.

The familiar tinge of anticipation and excitement start to creep through my body as I watch her tiny hands grasp my lover's swollen rod.

Every time I watch him press the head of his cock to the lips of some newly rescued victim, I feel the power of his cock as if it were attached to my body. This time the sensation is electrifying. Timidly, she parts her lips and starts to lick his shaft. We both stare at each other in bemused disbelief.

"It would appear the governor hasn't sent this one to school yet." I quip.

"Apparently not." He nods in reply.

I kneel down and place my hand on the back of her head.

"It's easy, just open wide and suck." I instruct her.

She glances at me as her jaw drops open. Before she can speak, his dick disappears past her lips. I hold her head fast as she gags, her poor little mouth stretched to the limit.

"Just relax your throat. That's it, just let his dick slide along your tongue and down your throat."

As I encourage her, I continue to push her head further down on his cock. I allow her to pull back just long enough to catch her breath then thrust her head back again. Feeling the power as his cock disappears into her mouth.

"I think we have a natural here." He stammers, obviously enjoying the gagging woman on the end of his dick.

Worked up in the excitement, I find myself grabbing his shaft, twisting and squeezing it. We take turns bobbing on the head and licking clean the length of his rod. He moans loudly. I can see the delight of having two women suck his cock all over his face. I break from his cock and let my fingers run down her back. As my hand crosses her waist and down her ass, she moans loudly. I suddenly remember that this is the first time she has ever been touched like this. So, I better make it count.

She shivers as my fingers cross her asshole, then continue past her quivering cherry. I press my index finger inside her unspoiled garden. Releasing a surprised shout of nervous pleasure, she pushes back against my hand wanting more. Trying desperately to concentrate on pleasing my man, she strokes his shaft as she drops her head down, moaning at the pleasure of being so gently penetrated by another person. I easily slide a second finger next to the first adding my thumb to play with her untouched clit.

"Oooooooooooo fuck me, ooooooo oh God, ooooooooo." She moans almost incoherently. I catch him smiling at me, obviously the pleasure of easily overpowering and seducing this little bitch is showing on my face. I don't care. I lean over and wink at him and I bite her ass cheek.

"Did I say to stop sucking, you little cunt," I bark firmly at her.

"No, ma'am," she whimpers in reply as she tries to catch her breath and return the waiting cock to her mouth.

"No, ma'am? Bitch, you call me master!"

"Yes, master. I will, master. I'm sorry, master," she manages to blurt out between thrusts of his cock.

 I easily slip a third finger in, stretching her tight little pussy, making her moan with delight. Wet juices run down my arm as I fuck her with my hand. She is powerless between us. I control her every thought and move, like a puppet. A simple twist of the wrist and her knees shake as she tries to scream around the rigid meat that is getting jammed down her throat! The power is intoxicating, and I want more. I pull my hand away returning it to her ass with a hard slap, leaving a clear red outline of my entire palm. I reach into my bag and pull out my little toy. The two of them don't seem to notice as I tighten the straps around my waist and thighs. Finally, he looks up and sees it—my strap on, my favorite toy. As I adjust it so the small knob slides into me, I stroke the end, almost able to feel the sensation through the massive tip down the sizeable shaft and back into my now dripping pussy.

"It's time for your spit roast, cunt! Put your ass in the air." He sternly directs her.

She tries to pull away from his cock to see what is coming in behind her, but he forces her head back down, gagging her until she follows his orders. I smack her ass again. She whines in pain and as I kick her knees apart, she is open to me. Vulnerable, wet, helpless—she can only manage a weak and pointless whimper in protest. She is begging me to be gentle as he holds her head up so we can both watch her face, contorting as I slowly force my dark tool past her quivering petals of her now broken flower. She cries out, screaming if only to help her cope with the enormity of the tool as I ruthlessly bury it deep inside her. As the sensation of her feeble cries carries through my toy and into my body, filling me with a sadistic pleasure, I push deeper, causing us both to gasp. Her, from the tearing pain, like a seem ripping down the length of her silken purse. Me, from the rush of power over this helpless creature. The harder I fuck her, the deeper my dark tool penetrates into my own deeply demented soul, coupling my desire to completely dominate this naive girl with my carnal cravings for total physical satisfaction. As she bows to my will and submits to my powerful thrusting, her body begins to rock into me. I can see it on her face; she is hating herself for wanting more. Her moans change, from cries for mercy to lustful gasps, begging me for more.

"This pussy belongs to me," I triumphantly declare!

She cries out. "Yes, yes, this is your pussy. Yes, master."

Arching her back, digging her nails into the shitty floorboards, I continue to pound her deeper into pathetic submission. I smile, knowing I have broken her will as well as her body. From this point on, she will always be a slave to my desires, a puppet for me to abuse. As each raised ridge of my tool stretches her labia and then disappears behind the engorged petal, her body trembles. My slow pelvic thrusts deliberate and smooth so I can savor the spectacle of each knobbed inch forcing its way inside her. I can see her body twist as I hit the limit of her depths, feel the pressure of my tool suddenly pressing back into me. My end of the device penetrating me, pressing on the upper recces across the ridges to the sensitive inner depths. The upper most portion rubbing against the hood of my clit electrifying the nerves throughout my body. She is too consumed by the power of my tool has over her body to be any use to my lover. Not to be left out, he moves to my side, squeezing my neck, making me gasp with delight. A trick he learned in a similar situation long ago. His kisses quickly move from lips down to my neck and shoulders, adding to my pleasure. My thrusts become faster as the excitement of him worshiping my body invigorates me. Feeling at the height of my power, I order him.

"Ruin her."

Without hesitation, he forces both of his thumbs into her anus, stretching and pulling it wide open. Her moans become cries as she tries to squirm away from this new pain. His grip on her is powerful, and he uses his strength to force her back against me. The sound of her skin slapping against the leather harness at the base of my toy is drowned out by her pathetic sobs and pleas simultaneously for us to stop and begging for more. Her body is covered in sweat, she slips back to her elbows as she tries to pull herself up onto her hands to try and minimize the angle my toy is penetrating her. Her struggling frame writhes on the floor in a puddle of her own sweat and juices. I lean forward, grabbing her hair, pulling her head back, biting her neck. The salty taste of skin like candy on my tongue.

My lover knows what's next. He releases her and moves aside to watch. With her hair in one hand and the other firmly grasping her hip I use all of my body to get as deep inside her as I can. Holding my toy in her depths I let my fingers slide from her hip to her clit. The pulsating button slips easily between my fingers. My rhythm follows the gyrating movements of her body and as her squeaks become silent and she starts to shake. I find the perfect pressure to make her explode. Her body convulses as her orgasm peaks. I feel the rush consume me. Every nerve in my body is on fire, the feeling of total power over her is intoxicating. The wave of pleasure crashes over me as the orgasm bursts inside me.

 I pull away, having climaxed on the power of complete control over her. For a moment I admire my handy work. A certain sense of satisfaction comes to me leaving her trembling, naked on the floor, trying to come to terms with the confused pleasure coursing over her trembling body.

I run my fingernails deep into his chest and whisper as I walk away, "Don't be too long."

I quickly remove my toy and redress in my gear. I can still hear her loud moans as I walk out the door.

"His turn." I think to myself as I throw my leg over the saddle of my bike, I look back and can see him over her, her arms and legs wrap around him as he forcefully enters her. The image of their gyrating bodies burring into my mind.

"Dirty girl," I mutter to myself, knowing she is in for a very long and satisfying night.

A small part of me feels sympathy for her. She is a perpetual victim in this world. I know we have saved her from a fate worse than death at the hands of the governor, and awoken her to the horrors she will face alone in this desolate and unforgiving place, but still deep down I hate that this is the only way to truly free her. Moreover, I hate what this world has made me become.

I can't deny, however, that the satisfaction, both physical and mental, of stealing away one of the governor's little dolls brings me a smile. I pull up my scarf, lower my goggles and ride off into this unforgiving wasteland. My mind is awash with memories of our night, and so many other nights like it, that my lover and I have shared before. Each one brings me closer to the end. With each victim rescued, I know we are getting closer to destroying the governor, and so I keep moving forward, keep searching for the next doll, each one draining his power a little at a time. I will bring him down one by one if I have to. I will never give up.

The dusty trail leads me away from the house and into the darkness. Like traveling out of a dream and into a nightmare. The trail leads me on toward the unknown and onto the next adventure. I have no idea just how close it is, and how far I was going to have to go to survive it.

Chapter 2

Painful Memories

Traveling at night is always risky—no roads to speak of—only well-traveled trails, unmarked and unwatched guide travelers between worn down outpost and far flung towns clustered around what little water there is to be had in this wasteland. For most, daily life is a struggle to gather what few resources can be found or salvaged, and they pay a heavy tax for "the privilege" of living behind the crumbling walls surrounding the towns. The last vestiges of a failed society. The disgust rises in my throat as I think about how easily people have given away their freedom, even their dignity, for the illusion of safety. An illusion propagated by the governor. As the miles roll away and the sun begins to sink dimly over the horizon behind me, my thoughts again drift back to the governor—how I once believed in the world he created, the fear of the dark he so passionately preached against.

That is, until they came for us. His goons showed up at our door demanding our family pay for the protection they so graciously bestowed upon us. They were the only ones we needed protection from. They demanded we pay either in gold or flesh. Our family was poor. We had no gold, so they took flesh. They attacked my mother first, violating her over and over. I could hear her screams for hours. My father tried in vain to protect her. They beat him mercilessly, his words became muffled and then quiet as the beatings drained the life from him. Eventually, all I could hear was the sound of the blows landing against his body, hollow thuds of wood against lifeless meat. I hid like a coward while they killed him. They took their time and beat him to death slowly, forcing him to watch as they took turns raping my mother again and again, until she couldn't even speak or cry out for help. They dragged the two of them off into the dessert. They tied his corpse to her naked body and left her exposed to the elements. It was a week before anyone found them, but it was too late. My mother died, tied to the corpse of my father, alone with only her shattered mind and her dead husband for company.

I wept. For the last time, tears would stain my dust covered cheeks. I wept until the dark returned. The next night they came back, the governor's men drunk, laughing as they pillaged our home, taking what little we had, burning anything they couldn't carry. Then, they found me. I was easy prey for them. Maybe fifteen bony, weak, emotionally destroyed, having seen the only two people I ever cared about so brutally ripped away. I tried to fight them, they just laughed and bound and gagged me, and threw me over the tank of one of their bikes.

I remember the largest of the men remarking "This one will make a nice prize for the governor." Seemingly pleased with himself for snagging such a trophy for his master.

I tried to struggle free only to be met with a rifle butt to my head. I blacked out, and when I awoke I was in a dark room, a large pool in front of me filled with water. The ripples reflected what little light there was across the walls and ceiling. Oddly I remember thinking what a waste it was. All that water was just sitting there when so many thirsty mouths toiled away for a mere canteen a day, my own mind clearly not grasping the reality of my situation. The throbbing in my head from the riffle blow had left me dizzy and completely foggy. I knew I was in trouble but could not even begin to grasp the nature of my surroundings. I couldn't help but focus on that pool. Like I was drawn to it, almost against my will. I just sat there and stared into it, trying to focus, trying to piece together how I got there.

Before my mind could clear, the governor emerged, a man seemingly immune to time. His pale skin pulled eerily tight over his massive frame. His bones seemed to almost push through his grey leather-like flesh, giving him a terrifying spiny profile. His face was sunken in, but his eyes seemed to emanate darkness. The kind of darkness that felt like it could swallow your soul. As he surveyed the room, his black lips split into a devilish grin, revealing his pointed teeth. A terrifying figure to behold. Upon seeing him, I was awash in the stories my parents told me about him. Stories about how hundreds of years ago a great society ruled the Earth and was destroyed by six people driven by greed and corruption. The governor was one of the six who created this wasteland on the ashes of that civilization. These six created a weapon that gave them absolute power and used it to kill millions. Then, they divided the world and the few remaining survivors amongst themselves to rule or destroy however they pleased.

I had always believed the stories were just fairy tales, told to fill the void when the old religions and governments had failed. A simple answer to explain all the world's suffering. After all, what kind of God would let his children wallow in such misery for so long. Now, as I watched this figure emerge from the pool, there was little doubt. Those were not just stories. The world was destroyed by those six people and this man was not only real but pure evil. I shuddered as he came to stand in front of me.

"Would you like to hear how I fixed the world?" he croaked in a distant voice, almost as if he was already bored by his own question. "That's usually the first thing people want to know when they meet me."

 It was then that I became aware we were not alone. I took a quick glance around and counted that there were twelve of us, and he was walking in a circle touching each one on the head as he went. I could see a green vapor being sucked from them. He was taking something—a piece of their soul, perhaps. I watched in horror as the life faded from their eyes and their bodies slumped over on a heap. I knew I should panic, that I should try to run, but like everyone else in the circle I could not move away from the pool. My mind was alert, but my body was frozen. The shimmering water had me hypnotized, or more accurately, paralyzed.

"I created a machine that could swallow your soul, your energy, even your memories and then it would give them to me," he spouted proudly.

 To whom he was speaking, I did not know. At first, it seemed he was just talking to himself to fill the time while he collected us all. Then I heard a brave voice speak up.

 "I heard you were just a janitor and the fucking thing backfired. That's why you're here, because you're a mistake and the others haven't found a way to kill you yet."

The voice was brave and unwavering, almost familiar. It came from a young man sitting across from me. He was not like us. His hands and feet were bound, his body cut and bruised. He had obviously put up more of a fight than the rest of us. He also seemed immune to the effects of the pool. In the dim light it was hard to make out details, but it was obvious he was a strong, well-built individual with rugged features that did not fit in with the rest of us sitting in the circle. He was different, and apparently, he was the one the governor was telling his story to. I was instantly mesmerized by him. I didn't know it yet, but he would be my future lover. For now, however, he just seemed to be a thorn in the governor's side—one the governor was anxious to eliminate. But not before he made him suffer. His words cut the governor like a knife and stopped him in his tracks. The governor composed himself and walked over to the man.

"Such a brave little man who thinks he knows the history of the world and yet is barely old enough to fuck," the governor hissed at him.

"I know enough. I know what it takes to sustain your miserable life, and I know how to take it away. Go ahead and try to take my power if you don't believe me," he bravely replied.

The governor reeled at the brazen confidence the man showed but did not shy away from the challenge. "Little man, I will do more than that. I will take your memories and replace them with the worst I can find. Your life will consist of one terrifying moment to the next, never knowing real from fake, reality from fiction."

"Just fucking do it then, you prick, unless this pointless monologue is part of your torture coz that might work." The man was almost smiling as he barked back at the governor.

 I caught myself laughing at his last remark. The governor shot me a look that turned my blood cold. Slowly, he placed his hand on the young man's head. I could tell by the contorted look on his face he did not like what he saw.

"No! This is not right; this is not what you're supposed to be!" Releasing his would be victim's head, the governor collapsed. The young man stood, breaking free of his restraints, and bound toward the door, grabbing my hand and pulling me with him out into the night.

Chapter 3

The Madam

Fuck, lights on my tail. I curse myself for being so sloppy. I know better than to let my mind drift like that out here. This is a dangerous place and there is little room for daydreaming on the trail. Reminiscing about the past only slows you down. How could I have been so sloppy? I pull off the trail after a sharp bend and stash my bike behind a large boulder. Climbing to the top, I lay prone, well hidden amongst the large rocks. The cool stone against my bare skin feels good against the hot wind blowing away my dust trail.

At first, I think I may have gone unnoticed. Then, I see the lights slow to a stop. They have picked up my trail and are following it toward me.

"Well, shit," I mutter to myself.

My chance to flee has passed. I will have to fight this one out. It won't be long now till they are within range. I pop the caps off my scope and steady my rifle. My side arm is locked and loaded. With any luck, it will be just one or two traders lost in the night. In my mind I know better, but still, it's nice to hope.

The vehicle cautiously picks its way along the trail, obviously following my track, looking for where I turned off, looking for me. So much for traders lost in the night. Safety's off. I tune the night vision on my goggles to maximize what little light there is and then adjust my scope. "*Damn.*" It looks like a band of scrappers. Truly the lowest level of scum this place has to offer.

These poor damned fools willing to risk a life of scavenging in the toxic ashes of the forgotten cities rather than live under the boot of the governor. Make no mistake, they are no better. On the contrary, some would say they are worse. Ruthless killers whose minds have been corrupted by the toxic fumes that still hang low over the shells of once mighty buildings. Their bodies suffer an even more gruesome and painful fate. Twisted and mutated. They barely even resemble humans anymore. They kill for fun and eat anything or anyone they can catch, not always having the courtesy to kill them first. I have no intention of joining them for dinner. As I slide the bolt closed, I can see they have someone tied up in their cage. It appears they already have a prize and a rare one at that. It's the madam from the brothel two towns back. I have seen her in passing on the rare occasion I was in town to trade. I guess I probably won't be going back there anymore. The town is most likely leveled. I shudder at the thought of the carnage these fuckers left in their wake. Scrappers rarely leave any survivors or for that matter buildings standing. Savage beasts, I can only imagine the hell that this woman has already been through, or the fate they have planned for her. Normally, I couldn't give two shits. People here are expendable and emotional attachments are guaranteed to get you killed, but this one is special. Something about her is drawing me toward her. My first instinct is to put a bullet through her skull to save her from the misery she is bound to endure at their hands, but I can't. I find myself mesmerized by her beauty and an overwhelming urge to save her comes over me. I guess I might as well pull her out of that cage. I train the crosshairs of my scope on the driver.

"Bullet, meet forehead," I whisper to myself as I gently squeeze the trigger. There's a bright flash and a loud report and I watch as the drivers head explodes through the lens. "I guess I'm in it now."

The rest scatter out into the surrounding brush. Taking cover behind whatever they can find. "Fuck, there's eight of them!"

I probably should have been a little more careful about counting them up before I let my pussy start making decisions for me. I squeeze the trigger two more times and two more drop into the sand.

"Three down, five to go," I muttered to myself.

I have found talking to yourself is an unfortunate side effect of spending most of your life alone. It does offer a certain amount of reassuring comfort in situations like these, however. Fuck, the other five have disappeared into the hills. Sneaky bastards. I have to get down there and get her out before they can regroup. I sling my rifle over my shoulder and sprint to the truck. No time to mess with the bike just yet. We will need it for our getaway, and I can't risk it getting shot up. The madam is bound and gagged but otherwise looks ok, which is surprising. Scrappers are known for their hostile treatment of future meals. I bust the lock on the cage and pull her out. As soon as she is free, I hear a bullet ricochet off the metal.

"Fuck, we gotta go!" I yell.

She nods and tries to stand but staggers and falls back to the ground. Of course, she can't stand. She's probably been in that cage for days with no food or water.

I drag her to the front of the vehicle. Another shot ricochets off my armor. I toss her my canteen. "Drink it and get ready to run."

She nods, tearing at the lid and ravenously drinking it down. I catch myself watching as some of the liquid spills from her lips down her chin and onto her bare, heaving cleavage. She catches me staring. Before I can respond she reaches under my skirt, pulls a pistol, and fires. Just behind me two more scrappers drop.

"Perhaps we can escape now and compare tits later?" she quips.

I stand, prepared to fight our way out, but there is just silence. The rest of those cowardly mutants have run away.

"Fucking cowards." I mumble under my breath angry at leaving this score unsettled.

"Well, that was exciting." The madam proclaims. "What's next?"

I turn to get a better look at my new prize. Her exotic features give her away. She is definitely not from around here. She has the porcelain skin and thin eyes of a visitor from Asia. Like every other woman I have meet from that land, she is petite but well proportioned, and for a woman of her former profession she has a surprisingly delicate frame and soft features. She certainly isn't dressed to be out here in the desert. Her calf boots have quite the heel, I would say at least six inches. No wonder she couldn't run away. I'm not sure I would even be able to walk in those things. Despite her diminutive stature, I am mesmerized by the sultry way her long legs are folded gently beneath her. The frilly blue fabric of her skirt barely covers the tops of her thighs and as I help her to stand, I can't help but to catch a glimpse of her panties, the same silky blue cloth, only with black lace around the edges. Her skirt seems to just barely cling to her body, cascading in the wind, ever teasing with subtle views of the tops of her thighs but never more. It rests lazily on her hips, falling slightly off one side. The contrast of her light skin and the dark fabric seems to be accentuated by the curves of her hips and the tight muscles of her stomach that draw neat lines from her abdomen up to her chest, where her ample bosom is peeking out of the bottom of another loosely placed strip of fabric laying across her breast. The fabric is the same blue and appears to be wrapped around her in a crisscross pattern, making an x and ending in her brown leather shoulder harness as it crosses her back and straps under her arms and back across her chest. It's a bold outfit for this place, but as I follow the curves of her hips up past her bosom, I can't imagine any other fabric that would be able to cling to such a perfect shape. Aside from the harness, her shoulders and arms are bare. Her neck is adorned with an intricate choker. A braided metal band at the top supports an interwoven mesh of bejeweled winding shapes that drape into a V at the crook of her neck. In the center, is a brightly colored pearl surround by a ring of rubies. The whole ensemble seems to cling to her skin like it is part of it, and it makes her already delicate neck seem even more fragile. The sharp features of her face seem to be softened by the strands of long black hair that have escaped from the messy bun on top of her head. Her thin but ample lips are painted bright red and I am only drawn away from them by her piercing brown eyes, perfect orbs hidden behind long lashes and dark eyeshadow that seems to draw my whole being into her gaze. I find myself lusting to consume this perfect specimen of a woman.

"We need to find a safe place to hide out." I place my hand on her hip, pulling her miniscule frame against mine. "Then we can get to know each other a little better." I tease, playfully, the adrenaline rush from the battle and the excitement of this beauty standing next to me making me feel giddy.

"Your place or mine?" I ask in my most playful tone. Trying to put her at ease.

She smiles, obviously pleased with this new course of events.

"I know a place. It's a bitch to get to, but we won't have any unwanted interruptions for, you know, getting to know each other," she playfully replies.

Her reply is everything I want to hear. Despite all my better judgement, I am ready and willing to follow her.

"Well, all right then, your place it is!" I say, taking her hand and excitedly leading her back to my motorcycle.

Her hand is small, almost doll-like, and our fingers lace together perfectly. Her soft delicate touch surprises me, and I feel myself wanting the sensation all over my body. I know this will end badly, just like everything else here, but for the moment I'm just enjoying the welcome touch of another woman, so soft and gentle in this harsh land. It is a rarity that I want to savor for as long as possible. She climbs on the bike behind me and pulls herself tight to me. I can feel the warmth of her body against mine. A familiar tingle of excitement travels down my spine as she leans in and wraps her arms around me, her hands finding the bare skin under my corset. The warm air from her breath makes the hairs on my neck stand up while she directs me where to go. As the words fall from her delicate lips, I am all consumed by my desire to taste them. I am barely able to hide my want as I can hardly contain my lust. Her soft voice fills my ears like a gentle sonnet whispered by a classical romantic poet from the past. She knows exactly what she is doing to me and very carefully brushes the hair away from my face. tucking it behind my ear before leaning in to give me more directions. With her head nestled on my neck she points to the forbidden mountain.

"It's up there. I can show you the trail, it's pretty well hidden."

It takes me a minute to snap back to reality. The forbidden mountain is past the edge of the inhabited part of this wasteland. Yet another place surrounded by mystery and death. I have never heard of anyone traveling to it and returning, much less hiding out there. Without giving it a second thought, I put the bike in gear and point the front tire towards the mountain. If she wants to lead me to my death, I think I might be oddly okay with that, just as long as she is holding me the whole way there. There is no logic to why I'm thinking this way. This intoxicating little woman has me completely bewitched, and I am loving every second of it.

Chapter 4

A Magical Place

We ride through the night and the next day. I keep expecting her bewitching trance to wear off and to come to my senses, but the more we travel together the more I want to feel and be felt by her. I am filled with a basic juvenile lust that is dangerously close to turning into an obsession. To be honest, I was really hoping to find a place a bit closer so we could just ravage each other as soon as possible, but I find myself unable to say no to her. Apparently, I am not the only one susceptible to her spell. Both times we stopped for gas and food, we somehow managed to leave without paying for either. Gifts for the pretty ladies the traders said, surprisingly generous for people with next to nothing to their names. Usually I have to negotiate prices at gun point this far out. With her though, she just smiled at them, and we were off, leaving them grinning and happy in our dust. My attention is drawn back to the trail as we reach the end of the know land and begin our ascent up the mountain. She holds me tighter as we begin to climb. The trail is quite rocky and I find myself struggling to keep up our pace. She doesn't seem to be bothered by the danger—In fact, I hear her laugh several times as we unexpectedly catch air. She's having fun. This woman, who only a day ago was on her way to be eaten by monsters, now clings to a perfect stranger for dear life who for all she knows has even worse intentions for her, and she is just having a blast as we tear along this God forsaken trail. I envy her carefree spirit and soon find myself grinning from ear to ear as I blast over bumps in the trail, making her squeal excitedly! You gotta hand it to her, this woman knows how to enjoy the moment.

Night falls and as we continue to follow the trail's twists and turns up the steep mountainside I slowly begin to wonder where she is leading me. Beautiful women often lead to trouble, and so far, this one has proven to be anything but the exception to that rule. Her arms squeeze tighter around my waist as the darkness makes the trail more difficult to navigate. Trouble or not, I enjoy the feel of her body against mine. It has been so long since I shared the company of someone I wasn't violating or having to lure into a trap. I had almost forgotten how nice it could be. I find myself again longing for her touch on my bare skin. In fact, I'm aching for it. Something about the building anticipation has awoken a deeper need inside of me. Is it some sort of trick she is playing on me or just my own inner desire to have some sort of meaningful connection with someone? Something that didn't involve violating another person against their will. I try to think back, to remember the last time I had felt so safe and secure in someone else's embrace, the last time I shared a moment with someone that made me feel this alive! Sadly, I couldn't remember a single instance. The darkness inside of me has corrupted even my brightest memories.

Suddenly, my lamenting is interrupted by something I have never seen before. The clouds of dust thin and then disappear as the trail climbs higher, and suddenly a sky full of... stars! Stars everywhere! I turn and gasp in awe. Just a never-ending majesty of tiny lights. I stop the bike and take off my goggles, slowly looking around to take it all in. Then I see it, glowing brilliant and white. The moon!

It is the first time I have glimpsed it without that awful red haze obscuring it, and it is brilliant. She laughs at my wonderment.

"So much for the tough girl act, huh? One little moon and you go all doe eyed on me."

I manage a feeble smile as I look back at her. "I have heard stories. I just never believed it was possible," I replied "It's just so breathtaking." Turning back to the moon, I can't help but get lost at the awesomeness of this expanse spread across the sky above me.

"Just wait till we get to the top," she whispers in my ear, holding her body tight to mine and letting her lips brush against my ear as she speaks. "If you think this is something, then the top will blow your mind." She gently kisses my neck and leans back, my signal to move on.

I take one last look around and then goose the throttle. If whatever is at the top is better than this, I want to get there fast. The trail continues to get steeper but now in the moonlight I can see clearly, and soon the top of the ridge looms into view. It takes all my focus to watch the trail and not the ever expanding sky as it seems to only get bigger and more awe inspiring the higher we climb. We reach the top of the ridge and as we go over the summit, I stop the bike again.

The top of the mountain is a huge caldera, several miles across and at the center of it a massive body of water at least a mile in every direction. Steep cliffs line the ridge, making it almost impossible to enter aside from the narrow trail in front of us that seems to wind precariously down into the lush green world below. It takes me a second to realize that the large green swath surrounding the lake is actually a forest made up of trees. I had seen pictures when I was a child but never a living one. It's hard to imagine so many of them, clustered together making an impenetrable looking wall around the water. In front of the trees several bushes of all sizes and shapes, and even grass could be seen—green and soft, like a blanket unfolded under the night sky. I want to lay on it and feel the soft fibers nestle my body. All of this seemed to be gently sloping towards the lake at the center. It is more water than I would have thought existed in the whole world. I knew of the oceans, great bodies of water so polluted with salt if you drank them you would die, but this was clean water seemingly filled with stars, and after a second, I am embarrassed to realize it is reflecting the night sky like a perfectly clear mirror. An occasional breeze ripples the otherwise still water, distorting the image, creating a whole new picture to baffle my mind. The breeze climbs the walls of the cliff and the cool air washes across my face. I close my eyes to soak in the refreshing sensation, feeling more alive than I ever have before. From here the world doesn't seem so harsh and unforgiving. I feel a warmth inside that has long been missing, just a small flicker, but it is there, nonetheless. I feel a sense of peace, nearly tranquility. I want to stay and take it all in. The magic of this place is intoxicating.

Before I can speak, she points to a spot near the shore. A flat sandy space that slopes ever so gently to the water. A beach. As we descend, the ground changes from wind swept rock to a soft lush green.

"It's so pretty!" I cry out.

She laughs.

I have never known anything to grow without artificial light aside from the gnarly sagebrush and scattered cacti that are hardy enough to survive the dust and dismal light down in the desert. I carefully creep down to the beach, not wanting to destroy these fragile little miracles. We reach the beach and I park the bike. As we both climb off, I pause for a second to take it all in. Rumors of an oasis like this have always been part of life in the wasteland but most of us put more stock in Santa Claus being real then a place like this surviving, much less thriving, way up here. The air feels cool, and the wind...has stopped. My passenger takes my hands in hers then leans forward and kisses me. Her soft lips gently press against mine, then her tongue brushes my lips and I let my tongue meet hers. It is magical, our gentle embrace under the stars, with tongues dancing and intertwining, her body softly pressed to mine. The moon seems to shine down just for us, bathing our bodies in the pale light—a magical moment in this impossibly perfect oasis. I don't want it to end, afraid if we let our lips part this whole world will come crashing back to the brutal soul crushing reality that awaits us below.

She breaks away first, taking two steps back and releasing her hands from my grasp. She smiles and as her fingers slip away from mine she redirects them, slowly unbuckling her dress and letting it fall to the sand. I am completely drawn in as she unveils herself to me. She continues to back away from me towards the water, dropping her clothing along the path. My eyes wonder across her naked body, completely bare aside from the choker on her neck. I lose myself, admiring the tone of her muscles, the smoothness of her skin, the way her long black hair flows gently in the light breeze, the shape and outline of each perfect curve. From her legs all the way to her glowing smile and sultry eyes, every step backward seems to accentuate another feature on her perfect form. The small tuft of hair above her mound trimmed neatly to the shape of a heart, the bounce of her breast as she moves, even the way her toes curl in the sand as she takes each step, inviting me forward. I trace the lines of her muscles away from her lady garden up past the curves of her hips to her breast. Perfect orbs with hard nipples begging for my attention. I pause only for another second to admire the shape of her body and the sensual grace of her movements as she bares herself completely in front of me. Quickly, I follow suit, and by the time we reach the water's edge we are both completely naked. Her pale skin glows softly in the moonlight. As our eyes meet, I become lost in hers, oblivious to the world around me. She gently starts to caress my arms. When her hands graze my breasts, I excitedly returned the favor. Her bosom is just large enough for each breast to perfectly fit in my hand and as I delight in teasing her nipples between my fingers, she does the same for me. I run one hand down to explore her exotic garden and find that aside from the very well-trimmed heart above her heaving mound, she is completely smooth. She moans with pleasure at my gentle touch as she leans in to kiss me. I can tell by her quivering petals she is desperate to have my fingers between them. I anxiously press forward to penetrate her, but she pulls away again, carefully pressing her finger to my mouth to stop my feeble protest.

"Up here we have all the time in the world. I want to show you how much I can please you." Her words have me dripping with excitement.

I nod in agreement, if only so I can get her finger in my mouth and slowly suck the tiny digit as she reluctantly pulls it away. She takes my hand and turns, revealing her backside to me, a perfect heart shape to match her coif that makes my mouth water. She leads me forward and as I take my first steps into the water, I am surprised at how pleasantly cool it is. There is a refreshing rush through my body with each step as we head deeper into this magical pool. The water is up to my thighs now. She gives me a kiss and then releases my hands as she lays backwards, allowing the refreshing liquid to envelope her body completely. I watch as she slowly sinks beneath the surface and I become more and more aroused, the cool sensation of the liquid washes over even more of my body as I follow her deeper into the lake. When the first ripples lap across the bare petals of my flower, I gasp, the pleasant sensation bringing to life in me an even stronger desire to have this woman's body against mine.

 Almost as if she can read my mind, she surfaces in front of me, her dripping skin glistening in the moon light. She takes both my hands and pulls me in for another kiss. I am lost in total bliss as she draws me in deeper, past my waist, up to my bosom. She encourages me forward and I watch as she again dives under the surface, her body a pale reflection against the dark water as she swims out further. I watch her every move, wanting to go after her. I hold my breath and go for it, submerging my body under the cool water, feeling it engulf me, then gently carrying me back up as I stand.

It then occurs to me I have no idea how to swim.

"Oh wow!" I state, exuberantly. It is an amazing new sensation to be completely submerged. The most I had ever had before was a small tub I could barely fit my body in, and even then, the water was dirty and warm. This feels clean and refreshing. She swims over and kisses me again, encouraging me to wade deeper.

All at once, she disappears under the surface, only to reemerge several yards away. She is floating effortlessly on the surface, encouraging me to swim to her. She quickly figures out by my hesitation I don't know how. She swims back to me. Standing next to me, I let her lower me into the water.

"Just lay on your stomach and move your hands like this," she explains, moving her hands in an awkward semicircle fashion.

I do as I'm instructed and find myself gliding weightlessly through the water. A little awkward at first but soon moving seamlessly.

"You're a natural." She beams at me.

The water invigorates me, washing away a lifetime of dust and grime and melting away the horrendous memories of my dark and violent past, at least for now. We swim out deeper into the lake, intertwining our bodies, pulling each other into a sensual embrace then breaking free to swim away— like an aquatic dance. Laughing, splashing and allowing ourselves to relax and actually have fun under the intoxicating moonlight.

Eventually she swims to shallow water, and when I catch her she pulls me into a passionate embrace. The waist-deep water feels warm now as the cold night air blows across our naked bodies.

Cold night air, I never could have imagined. My mind is instantly drawn back to the naked figure entangling her body with mine. My senses feel overloaded. Between the cool air, the refreshing water, and her warm naked body pressed to my skin I am in heaven. Even in my wildest dreams I never imagined how complete the feeling of being truly happy could be. Her arms are wrapped around me, holding me to her, our lips locked together. This is not like the gentle kisses we shared earlier in the night, this is a hungry, deep lustful kiss full of want and desire. I desperately cling to her body, wanting to feel more, wanting to touch every inch of her at once, to be inside her and have her inside me. Her delicate ladylike posturing is gone. Lust has consumed us both. I pull at her hair as she finds my nipples with her teeth. We stumble backwards onto the beach, only our feet still left in the water. The soft warm sand coddles our bodies as we roll and tumble trying to pull each other ever impossibly closer, feverishly longing for a more complete embrace.

"Yes, yes!" I hear myself moaning almost without realizing it.

I can't control this desire burning inside me, this overwhelming unceasing need to feel her, taste her. I want her to consume me completely. She's on top of me, her weight barely anything at all. I reach to pull her down to my lips, but she smiles and pulls away. I drop my arms to my side as she gently kisses my neck and then chest, her lips leaving a warm trace from each kiss before fading into the night air. I delight at her hands pinning my shoulders to the sand. I relax into her control and gently follow her kisses down my body with my fingertips. I can feel her hot breath on my stomach as she shifts her body lower, her strong legs pressing mine apart. I give into it and part my legs slightly. She heeds my signal and runs her hands up my thighs. I arch my hips in anticipation. I'm shaking. I need to feel her inside me. Her fingers brush over my labia and press against my hood. The sensation is amazing. I moan in approval. She lets one finger slowly slide back down, gently parting the lips. It's all I can do to keep from grabbing her hand and shoving it inside me. She reaches up and grabs my neck, pulling herself up to me, and kisses me as she finally lets her finger disappear inside me. The rush runs through my entire body, like an electric spark of pleasure emanating from deep inside, flowing outward to the tips of my fingers and toes. Each time she enters me another spark. My mind is spinning— another spark, they are coming in waves now. I can't focus. How is she doing this?

Another wave, bigger this time as she fills me with a second finger and lets her thumb dance on my clit! I want to reciprocate but all I can do is dig my nails into her back, another wave.

"*Oh, God*" I think.

The pleasure is so much more intense than anything I've felt before! Another wave! I hear loud moaning. It takes a second to realize I am the one moaning. I don't care, I go with it. I let go and lean into it. Her lips—oh, God, how good they feel all over my body. The water gently washes our legs as we move together, like it's washing away all my fear and hate and dark memories. Her lips feel like warm light beaming onto my skin wherever they touch! Another wave, I am ready to give myself to her completely. Another wave! I feel like I'm floating. Another wave, and I just want more of her inside me!

The warm soft sand cradles my back in an unexplainably comfortable way. My body is completely relaxed as her lips move from mine, down my neck, her fingers still working their magic. The waves of pleasure are growing. The further down I feel her soft kisses on my body the more intense each wave becomes. God, her tongue is teasing my nipples and she sucks in my breast, still teasing with her tongue. I want more, but all I can do is dig my fingers into the sand behind me and moan loudly as wave after wave of ecstasy crashes over me. My hand finds her smooth silky hair. I grab what I can, I need more of her touching me! She slides further down, kissing around my belly button. My legs shake uncontrollably. I feel the unmistakable tinge of an orgasm growing inside me. I want it, but I don't want this to end. I hear myself repeating

"Yes, baby. Please, baby!"

I don't care and I can't control it anyway. I'm too lost in the moment. I feel her head between my thighs. Without hesitation, I spread my knees as far as I can get them. Oh, her lips, her wonderful talented lips, are on my inner thigh, alternating from leg to leg, getting closer with each kiss. It's uncontrollable now, my fingers pull at her hair. Her breath is teasing my lips, teasing me to my very core. I can feel each hot breath against my clit. She kisses the hood gently and pauses, letting her lips delicately touch my sensitive folds while I gasp. Then I feel her tongue start to trace along the sides of my vagina, starting at the outside of my lips, slowly working their way around to the top. My whole body is shaking uncontrollably now,

 Each wave brings the orgasm closer. She presses her tongue against my pussy and with a few gently flicks I explode! It comes as a flash of light—for a second, I swear I can see the stars dance, an amazing rolling sensation of indescribable pleasure carries throughout my entire body. Every muscle contracts, pulling the sensation back in, then releasing as it explodes outward followed by a long wave of euphoria.

"Oh, God, I've never cum like that," I stammer.

"Baby you're in for a treat tonight!" she says, smiling back at me while gently pulling my knees back apart. Before I can catch my breath, her tongue is deep inside me. I can feel each little flick travel through me. She lets her tongue carefully return to my clit, still sensitive from the last orgasm. As she slowly places just the tip under my hood, I feel her work down onto my clit, letting my body dictate the pressure by my heaving hips. The overwhelming waves return, and the rush is again building inside me. She sucks my clit, pulling it deep into her mouth and pressing it tight between her teeth, flicking it with her tongue. As her fingers slide back into me my knees snap closed uncontrollably. She doesn't miss a beat, instead she works into me harder. I pull her head tighter against me, needing, wanting more. The explosion is building, I'm past the point of trying to understand or control it. I embrace it and let it build through my entire body. I relax my legs letting her pull them apart, using both hands to spread me open and get her tongue impossibly deep inside me. The stars start to shake as she continues the steady rhythm of her hands, and the impossibly intuitive caresses from her mouth rock my body over and over. I open my mouth to scream but no sound comes out. I can only manage a small squeak as the second orgasm rocks my body, this time in a long wave starting deep inside me from my very core, and then another, and another! I try to mutter "stop" but yell "FUUUCCCK" instead as she buries three fingers in me while sucking my clit. My body rocks uncontrollably, locking her face and hands in place as the orgasm races through me. I feel it in every muscle, every digit, even in my bones. My mind swirls as the feeling spreads out of me like a lightning bolt until my body collapses from fatigue, releasing my captor to breathe. The world is spinning as the last wave ebbs and the mere touch of her finger on my thigh gives me uncontrollable aftershocks. It takes several deep breaths before I can manage words.

"Oh, fuck, baby! I mean wow, I never...."

She quiets me with a kiss, her lips still wet and swollen from pressing against my labia with such pressure.

"You have the sexiest orgasms ever." She compliments me with a smile.

"Oh, my GOD!" I repeat "You set the bar pretty high, but I think I'm up for the challenge. Just let me catch my breath."

She laughs, very pleased with herself. Tracing her fingers across my still shaking body.

As my body settles and my senses return so does my lust for her. My desire to please her comes from a place inside me I am not familiar with. I want to—no I need to—satisfy this woman just to please her, and I want nothing in return. She seems content to just lay by my side, casually caressing me and exchanging gentle kisses, but the fire inside me is growing and I have an uncontrollable desire to consume her, to taste her on my tongue, to feel her wetness with my fingers, to have her body shake the way she shook mine. She leans in to kiss me again only this time I pull her tight to me. Our gentle kiss has turned to a passionate embrace, and she willingly gives herself over to me. The soft feel of her tongue inside my mouth excites me further and I slip my own past her teeth, wresting hers biting her lower lip, pulling, then pressing my lips against hers again and again. The taste of her is sweet, and I can't get enough. I pull her hair back, exposing her neck. I kiss and bite and nibble, becoming more aggressive with each moan of pleasure she emits from her body. I push her onto her back and roll on top of her, easily pinning her tiny body beneath mine. Gripping her hands above her head with one hand, grasping her neck tightly with the other. Her body rocks with want, trying to grind against me but I have her legs pinned to the sand with mine. As I look into her eyes, I can see she is asking for me. She begs me to take her. Her soft voice just sultry notes of desire as she pleas for me to ravish her.

"Please, please take me. Please, I'm yours. You can have me any way you want me, just take me!"

Her pleas turn to moans as I spread her legs with mine. She doesn't try to resist, and I easily expose her to me. I release her hands but hold fast her neck as I slide my body further down hers. I know what she wants, but this is a game of anticipation and I am going to have her dripping long before I penetrate her. My mouth finds her nipples, hard and waiting. I carefully bite each one in turn, delighting in how she squirms beneath me. She grabs my free hand and begins slowly sucking each finger, her moans barely able to escape around them. The sensation of her wet mouth on my digits is exquisite. I want more, but I am here to please her now. I will just have to wait my turn. I pull my hands away from her, flipping her over to her stomach and pulling her hips up to my face. She tries to get on her elbows, but I push her back down, leaving her wildly vulnerable and exposed to me. With one hand holding her shoulders down I slide the other across her back and down her ass, letting my fingertips graze her most sensitive areas. She cries out "Oh, fuck yes, please!"

I continue to tease her, running my hands up and down her thighs and across her mound, pressing into the areas next to her lips but never penetrating her. Her legs are shaking, betraying her want for me, and I delight at how wet I am making her. I blow gently up and down the length of her lips, carefully separating them just enough to allow my hot breath to reach her inner petals. She digs into the sand with her fingers. Her whole body is shaking as I spread her completely open and let myself taste the first drops of her juices as I penetrate her ever so slightly, running my tongue from coccyx to clit, slipping neatly back into her vagina, mixing her juices with my saliva. Her taste is extraordinary. I press my tongue deeper into her to get more of her flavor in my mouth until my whole face is pressed into her. My fingers work her clit while my tongue is busy inside her, then I pull back her hood to allow my mouth better access to her magic button. She cries out loudly as the tip of my tongue flicks her wildly, pressing in hard then working it in every direction my mouth has the ability to reach. Her legs are shaking uncontrollably, and her body is rocking wildly but I hold her tight to my face. Her cries are unintelligible now and as I slip a finger into her dripping wet hole, she begins one long series of moans, each followed by a body shaking shudder.

I have to pause to catch my breath and let my fingers take over where my tongue had ruled.

"Do you like it, baby? You want more?" I tease.

"Yes, baby. Yes, I want more, I want more. Please don't stop, give me more baby!" she cries in reply.

I flip her over onto her back and dive back into her pussy. My new angle allows me to suck her clit and slide two fingers easily inside her, pressing her from the inside along the path my tongue is following from the out. As I let her clit slide past my teeth, she grabs my head with both hands, forcing my face hard into her, crying out for me not to stop. I rotate my hand inside her and press my thumb into her anus, her dripping pussy having soaked it, allowing me to slip in easily.

The added sensation drives her over the edge, and now she is bucking wildly, unable to control herself as I send powerful waves of pleasure through her with each flick of my tongue and twist of my hand. She locks her legs against my head as she rocks back and forth. I bury my fingers inside her, holding her fast as I tease her clit even more aggressively with my mouth—wide tongue strokes and powerful flicks followed by long licks and sucking her into my mouth, holding her gently with my teeth.

"Oh God, Oh God, Oh FUUUUUUCK!" she cries loudly.

I can feel both her holes contract around my fingers repeatedly as her taste changes from juice to cum. I look up her body to watch as the orgasm ravages across her and leaves her breathless. Every muscle in her tiny frame tightens and slowly releases with each wave as it washes over her. I hold my hands fast and let my tongue gently tease her until the last wave has passed and she collapses breathless back against the sand. I slowly withdraw myself from her and she pulls me up to her, kissing my wet face, an astonished and satisfied look on her face.

"Oh, my God, thank you," she manages to whisper to me before dropping her arms limp into the sand, a satisfied smile painted neatly across her glowing face. I lay down next to her, exhausted but quite pleased with my performance. I watch her chest heave as she tries to catch her breath, we don't speak, just the occasional "wow" slips past her lips as she lays helpless next to me. I pull her close to me and she eagerly entangles her limbs with mine, the warmth from our bodies contrasted by the cool night air. For a moment, everything is perfect.

We lay basking in the moonlight, our naked bodies spent and sprawled on the sand, almost unable to believe this is all still real I marvel at the site of her body intertwined with mine. We kiss softly, just enjoying the afterglow. The sun is starting to rise on the horizon and the black night sky is giving way to deep blue. Her fingers trace the curves of my body while I use mine to desperately hold her tight to me. As we watch the sun rise over the ridge and the sky turn an impossible light blue,

I marvel at the beauty of it all. Just to see the sun rise unimpeded by the dust would be enough, but to have her lying beside me as the suns first warm rays kiss our skin is almost too much to comprehend. I try my best to not act surprised at how bright and clear everything is. She very politely ignores my "ooos" and "ahhs" at every new wonder revealed to me by the morning light. The warmth from the sun slowly rouses our bodies, and I know soon I will have to let her go.

She pulls my face back to hers, not saying anything, just staring into my eyes.

"What?" I ask, sheepishly

"I was just thinking that I was getting a little bit hungry. I thought you might be, too," she replies, coyly.

"I hate to admit it, but I'm starving. Do you think there is something to eat up here? My saddlebags are empty, but I would rather starve than leave this place for something as pointless as food," I reply.

I can tell by her smile she has yet another trick up her sleeve. She slides her body on top of mine and gives me a long kiss, then brushes the hair away from my face so she can stare into my eyes again.

"Girl, have I got a surprise for you."

Suddenly, I notice a strange light coming from the woods behind us. I sit up with a start. She grabs my hand reassuringly, helping me to my feet. I look into her eyes and see they are filled with excitement and mischief.

"Why do I feel like this is going to be awesome?" I ask.

"Because everything I do is awesome," she jokingly replies.

As we turn our bodies toward the light, I can see a small figure approaching.

She whispers in my ear, "I have so many more wonderful things I want to show you!"

The figure is a man, slight in stature. His clothes are foreign to me. I've never seen anything like them. A tight fabric stretched over his tiny body accounting for what appears to a total lack of physical prowess and a very ...well... "cute" boner,

for lack of a better way to describe it. In his arms
are two towels and two robes. The robes look to be
made of silk and as the man trods carefully onto the
sand I can see his feet are tiny and bound in several
layers of different color cloth strips. I catch myself
staring curiously at this little man, completely
forgetting my already strange surroundings or the
fact that I am totally naked.

He tries to attend to the madam first, attempting to
dry her body and wipe the sand from her skin
before she angrily shoos him away. After a quick
tongue lashing in what I am guessing is an Asian
language, the little man turns his attentions to me.
Quickly, but with an almost effeminate grace, he
has me clean and dry. He then offers me the robe,
averting his eyes to my naked body, which seems
silly as he just had his hands all over it. As the silky
fabric slides over my skin I feel myself
invigorated—sexually excited, even. Somehow, the
fabric is making my whole body feel smooth, soft,
sensual. She notices my reaction to the fabric and
giggles.

"It's nice, right?" she asks

"It's amazing," I reply. "What is it? Some kind of super fabric you guys discovered over there or something?"

"Sort of. It's real silk, but different from most the stuff they try to pass off as silk around here. It's actually been around for thousands of years; we just don't trade it with Wastelanders."

Her reply makes me pause. I had never heard the term Wastelander before. Mostly, it had never occurred to me that there was any place that was all that different from the Wasteland. We were always told that the other regions were harsh unforgiving places, just like here. Even the travelers and traders that came through would remark about how messed up the rest of the world was. Now, however, hearing this place referred to as Wasteland by an outsider, the thought crept in that perhaps other places like Asia might be different. One thing was for sure, at the very least they had enough water to learn to swim.

"Wastelanders?" I asked, a little inquisitive, and a little offended.

"Right, you don't know about the other regions. I sometimes take it for granted that I have been able to travel to so many places, and I often forget that he never lets people leave here. Why don't you come inside, and I will show you what I am talking about."

I feel slightly offended by her nonchalant attitude to ruining my world view. After all, she was stuck here, too. How great could these other places be? I quickly brushed it off, however. After what we shared last night, I really didn't care if she talked down to me a little. She wants to be with me and I want to be with her, so why would any of the rest of it matter?

She takes my hand. I only hesitate for a second. My baser instincts are yelling in my head that this is all too much, that it is all too good to be true. A small part of me is actually wondering if this is some elaborate plot by the governor. I shake off my doubts quickly, knowing this goes far beyond what happened in the lake. I trust her implicitly, and I feel like she trusts me too. Instincts be damned, I feel I should give the madam the benefit of the doubt. So, I follow her into the strange light and another world.

The light as it turned out is coming from a large door, well hidden by the thick vegetation around it. As we step inside, the little man closes the door behind us, and I hear the locks securing it, heavy and solid. There's no way I am leaving here by my own accord now. Still, I feel safe with her holding my hand. She barks more instructions I don't understand, and the little man disappears behind another door. The room itself is quite large—you could easily fit one hundred people in here. The lights are like the ones I had seen at the governor's cave when I was taken all those years ago. She flicks a switch and the room is washed in a warm white glow, no shaking or rolling or trying to light things like the magnet lights and crappy lanterns I was used to. They are bright as well, lighting up every corner of the room which was decorated in keeping with what I assume are the madam's cultural traditions.

Large bolts of cloth hang from the ceiling, obscuring the brightly painted walls, while soft pillows and backless couches are scattered in a semi-orderly fashion about the floor. The floor itself is covered in a plush white carpet that feels like I am walking on a cloud. As we move around the room, I notice huge works of art adorning the walls between the fabric and in several places' bookshelves, two stories high, packed with actual books.

I can't resist. I pull one down and run my hand across the cover. Moby Dick. I had a paperback copy as a child and read it over and over. It was one of the few books I had ever seen, much less read. After all, books are hard to come by here. The governor has worked hard to keep his people dumb and uneducated. The masses are easier to control that way. Most of the things I read are either the repair manual for the bike or journals I have taken off the people I killed or violated. This is almost overwhelming. She gives my hand a gentle tug, pulling me away from this mesmerizing collection and leading me to the back of the room where four large screens are mounted high on the wall. I have seen screens like these before. The Governor keeps one in every town, so people are forced to see his face and hear his message when he goes on his hate-filled speeches and tirades, or his orders to hunt some poor soul down for a pitiful bounty. These appear to be nicer, or at least cleaner. From behind yet another door the little man appears with a tray full of fruit and cheeses.

"Oh, my God!" I exclaim,

Fresh fruit and cheese are a rare delicacy and I rudely reach for a handful without asking. I get why she was talking down to me earlier, this place is nothing like the rest of Wasteland. The madam doesn't seem to notice, and after a few mouthfuls I am able to compose myself.

"Something to drink—beer, wine, tequila?" she asks.

I nod and the little man sets the tray down only to disappear behind the door. As we settle ourselves on some large overstuffed pillows in front of the screen, the little man returns with two glasses and a decanter filled with a dark red liquid. I could not remember the last time I had seen wine, let alone got to taste it. As the glasses are poured and distributed, I manage to wait for the madam, this time as we both take our first sips together.

"I hope you don't mind red wine. We should probably save the tequila shots for later," she playfully suggests.

I nod in agreement. Truth be told, I can't care less what she was serving. I have a feeling it will all be wonderful.

"Ah, that's the stuff' I was getting tired of drinking the dirt water and cheap whisky all those towns are full of. A girl's got to have something a bit frilly once in a while too!" she proclaims.

I nod, enjoying the warm feeling on the back of my tongue as the sweet burgundy colored liquid fills my mouth and flows down my throat. We drink and talk, reflecting on the differences between our two worlds. That is what little she will tell me about her world. I can tell she is definitely hiding something, and it is eating away at her. I know she wants to tell me. After several decanters we are both fairly well-lit, and her mood turns surprisingly serious.

"So, how much do you know about the fall of man?" she asks.

"Just that it was a long time ago and somehow the governor got super powerful from destroying the world," I reply.

She scrunches her face up in what I assume to be a frown. Even when she is trying to be serious, she is just adorable. I can tell by the way she is shifting in her chair that she is trying to get the courage up to tell me something. I touch her hand gently, reassuring her.

"Well, I would like to tell you the rest of the story and then ask you for your help."

I tilt my head inquisitively. As she speaks the screens in front of us came to life, and for the first time I am seeing images of the world before the fall. There were so many people, every picture and video are just full of them.

"About two hundred years ago, the Earth's population hit ten billion," she begins, "too many people for the planet to support. Each person consumed resources at a voracious rate. Every new technology that was developed to combat this waste only seemed to make the problem worse. The ecosystem was dying, the air barely breathable— even the sun was getting blocked out by pollution. Five people came together with a solution. At first, they were considered mad genocidal maniacs. At the time, everyone thought that every life was special. They even worked to save the lost, sick, and dying using tremendous amounts of resources just to buy them a few more days, hours, or sometimes even seconds."

She sounds like she is reciting a speech or reading off a card. I know her monotone voice is just her way of keeping back the emotions she is feeling. It must be hard to relive this information in such vivid detail. I sit next to her holding her hands. They are trembling.

"The Five saw things differently. They saw that a population one-twentieth the size of the current population could live and prosper on this planet for thousands of years to come. Their plan was simple in concept. Build a device that could eliminate the human problem without destroying the world they live in. In the end, building the device was the easy part—a machine that absorbs the very power that gives us life, everything from the energy that holds cells together to the energy we use to store memories. Carefully selected individuals and groups were moved to safe zones and the machine collected the power from the rest, quick and painless.

The Five saw it as their duty to recreate a society with the ones they saved. So, they divided the world into different regions, each region focusing on a different discipline that would benefit not only mankind but the Earth, so it could be healed."

"The five regions are: Ocean, Earth, Air, Science, and Culture. The Ocean region is located on the islands in the Pacific, a tremendously large body of water to the east of us. The Earth region is located on a massive continent that used to be known as Africa, halfway around the world from this place. The Air region is centered throughout the high peaks of the Andes, a mountain range in what used to be the continent of South America several thousand miles south of here, the region for

Science, located in Europe, another huge land mass far to the west. And the region for Culture, is in Asia, often considered the largest land mass of them all. It sits on the other side of the Ocean region."

"There was a sixth need that arose, however. Even amongst the best and the brightest there will always be people that want to break the rules—murder, lie, cheat, rape, and steal. The governor was created to oversee this sixth region, the Wasteland, that was placed here in the desert wastelands of what used to be North America. With natural boundaries on almost all sides, a little bit of weather modification was all that was needed to contain those that wanted to live outside the law. At first it went well. The governor doled out his own brand of justice and peace reigned in the other regions."

"I guess this is where you tell me what went wrong?" I ask.

"Well, yes, the machine The Five created works by absorbing the power of the people it's around and then storing it for later use for everything from electricity to medicine to food. Absorbing the power of another person is like a fountain of youth, it rushes through your body replenishing your own energy on all levels. Thereby, with the right amount of power, one could live forever. The drawback is, it only lasts for a short period of time. Anywhere from a couple of years to a couple of hours depending on the person's power levels when it's collected. The governor figured out that if he collected it from people without a dark spot on them, he could get more power from them."

"Wait, what does a dark spot have to do with it?" I ask

"People with a traumatic past tend to create dark power which is really only good for electricity, and power for machines. The dark power doesn't repair your body. Instead, it leaves you hollow, broken and rotten at your very core. Your lust for power will control you and no matter how much you get you'll always want more."

"Well that explains the dolls he is always keeping hidden all over. That asshole is just using them as batteries!"

"Exactly," she replies.

Chapter 5

A Plan Forms

My mind is racing as I try to absorb all this new information. On the screens horrible images and videos keep flashing in quick succession, like a time lapse for the end of humanity. I feel my hands shaking, and for the first time in as long as I can remember tears fall down my cheeks. I am caught off guard by the rush of emotion and as hard as I try to pull it back, it surges forward out of me.

"What about me, what about my parents?" I cry out. "What did any of us do to deserve this?"

My question hangs in the air as she pulls closer to me. When she takes me into her arms I collapse into her embrace. The floodgates open and tears stream down, soaking her chest. I hold onto her tightly as the sobs pour out of me in bursts. The warmth of her bosom on my face is comforting. Instead of anger, I just feel sadness—another new and confusing emotion I have been able to push down for longer than I can remember. I feel her body convulse. She is crying with me. Something about the sharing of suffering eases the pain, and I am able to compose myself after several moments. She wipes the tears from her face and continues.

"For a while, the Wasteland was only for those who were being punished. Once the governor discovered he was able to harness the power for his own selfish gains, everything changed. The other five tried to wipe him out, but he is smart. He went underground deeper than thought possible. He then figured out how to transfer dark power to his lackeys, the henchmen this land has come to fear, making them twice as strong as a normal man and totally dependent on his generosity to live. He built up a small army and wiped out any link to the world outside the wastelands. Everyone left here was trapped, forced to submit to him or face annihilation. Some tried to escape, risking death trying to cross the high mountains with no protection and no gear. It proved a pointless endeavor. The Five tried to pull out as many as they could, but the governor's attacks on the rescue parties grew more and more violent and his retribution to those they couldn't get out became so brutal the rescues were abandoned. Other attempts were made to try to wipe him out—everything from modifying the weather to an invasion by a big mechanical army. He survived them all using the power he absorbed or could steal to fight off all of their attempts."

"So, the wind, the sand, the destroyed cities and mutant scrappers?" I ask, softly.

"All results of the war. For fifty years, The Five tried everything. Finally, when they couldn't stand the suffering any longer, they declared a truce. The governor would be confined to the Wastelands with control of all its people and The Five would respect his borders as long as he did not try to expand or become more powerful." she paused to let it sink in.

It dawns on me that my family was doomed just from getting trapped in the wrong place at the wrong time.

After a moment she continues, "That was one hundred years ago. The Five have always kept people here to make sure he honors his end of the treaty. About twenty years ago we discovered his dolls that he is using to increase his power. To what end we don't know, but they knew it was time to act. With an in-depth knowledge of where he was keeping his dolls, they decided it was too good an opportunity to pass up, so the council of The Five came up with a new plan—turn all his potential sources of positive power to dark power. And so, they began sending us here to find and destroy his dolls."

"So, your plan is basically to kill the governor by raping people to death? All those poor people's lives brutally ruined to fix a mess you created! It seems a bit much," I yell, confused and embarrassed at my own willing participation in so much pain.

I can see she senses my rising anger.

"The council has been trying to kill the governor for the last two hundred years. This is the closest they have come. It is horrible for the victims, but their sacrifice will free so many more. You know that, you have helped us with much less information then you have now and no proof whatsoever! This was thought to be our last option, until we found you."

I look up to see her staring into my eyes, her hands holding mine firmly, that weird glimmer of hope in her expression. I know she's right. I have done horrible things, things that I shudder to think of. What proof did I have? None really. Just the word of a psycho that pulled me out of a cave. It was his promise that we could destroy the governor together that started me down this path, but until now I never even questioned why. I just wanted to cause as much pain as I could to try and relieve my own.

I sigh. Deep down I know I am going to help, I just don't want to admit it so easily.

"Well, I haven't been able to say no to you yet. What's the plan?"

Her face lights up at my reply, and she throws her arm around me and kisses me—a strong, deep, passionate kiss!

"Well, Well, Well, perfect timing as usual."

The male voice from behind us is familiar. I turn and see him, my lover, standing in the middle of the room. He is also wearing a silk robe, barely covering his plentiful manhood and open at the chest.

He does like to show off his scars, I think to myself.

"Do you mind, heathen?!" the madam barks at him. "We were having a moment!"

"Don't mind at all. In fact, I think I might sit here and watch!" he quips back.

He drops onto one of the couches, and a grin from ear to ear paints his face. The small man brings him a tray of fruit and wine.

"What's up, my little boner buddy?" he asks, offering his hand up for a high-five.

The small man smiles meekly, then scurries away.

"I love that little guy, even though he always leaves me hanging. We got to get him a better suit, though. Dude got mad camel toe showing."

"Seriously, I'm trying to explain what's going on and her role in bringing down the governor!"

my lover is unshaken by the madam's stern tone.

"Allow me. It will be much faster and then you two can go back to whatever lady business was happening when I came in!"

Before she can reply, he has moved next to me and has one finger pressed to mine

"we," pointing to the madam and himself, "aren't from around here. We are volunteers sent by the council to fulfill the will of the original Five and end the governor's reign of terror and bring peace and prosperity and possibly even fuzzy bunnies to this land!"

His sarcastic tone brings a noticeable chafe to the madam.

"The two of us were each given the ability to both give and take power from people—her the light power, and me the dark power. We use this power to manipulate people into telling us where all of the gov's dolls are and then when we find them, we turn their power to dark so that they are useless to the Gov. However, you are different, and you presented us with a special opportunity. You are one of the rare people who can manipulate both powers and therefore we can use you to poison that ass hat then we can take all his shit! Any questions?" He is standing on the couch at the crescendo of his argument, gesturing wildly like he is grabbing armfuls of riches, seemingly quite pleased with his performance.

"Well, yes actually, I have quite a few," I respond. "For starters, what the actual fuck? Secondly, I think you need to elaborate a little more on this light and dark shit. It sounds like something out of a kid's nightmare."

He almost spits out his wine. The madam shakes her head and tries to calmly explain it to me.

"We use the term power, but it's really all just energy. The light flows into your body, like when you eat or have an orgasm. It gives you a euphoric feeling, but it can also nurture and heal you. The dark flows from your body, leaving you angry and tired. We went light and dark to make it simple. The scientific terms are much too lengthy to use in polite conversation."

The madam's word sink in, but she can tell by the vague look on my face I'm not buying it.

"Look," I say. "I got involved with this taint tickler because he pulled me out of the governor's cave and then told me about how I could help him ruin the governor's dolls for revenge, not to play lights on lights off for freedom or whatever is going on so please, for fucks sake, tell me what the plan is and don't say I'm going to have to suck that cock sucker's dick to kill him, cause that's where I draw the line."

At this point my lover is rolling on the floor laughing. "I told you, this chick is awesome!"

The madam shoots him a stern glance, to no effect.

"Here, kiss me," she insists.

Not wanting to pass up an opportunity to feel her lips against mine, I lean forward. She grabs the back of my neck. She quickly parts my lips with her tongue. I pull her head tighter to mine as our tongue's roll together between our mouths. Her smooth skin passes under my fingers as I reach for a handful of her hair and let the other hand fall to her breast. Before I can pull her robe away, I feel an overpowering warmth deep within me. My whole body tenses as the warmth turns to an explosion, releasing all my muscles with a wave of ecstasy, leaving me shaking and tingling all over.

"Oh, my God, did I... I just came!" I exclaimed "From a kiss. I mean, it was a great kiss but..."

She smiles as she pulls away. "That's the power of the light."

My lover, now standing next to me, his robe doing little to hide his excitement, speaks up. "That's nothing, she can do that from across the room to most dudes."

The madam sighs in disgust.

"So, what does the dark do, then?" I ask.

A serious pall falls about the room. The two make eye contact, and she nods to give him the go ahead.

"I'm sorry in advance," he says mournfully. Then, with the lightest touch, he pulls my finger to his lips and kisses it ever so softly. I instantly slap him. The anger is uncontrollable, like every bad memory and every horrible thing I have ever seen, done, or had happened to me exploding in my mind all once. My mind is pure rage—all I can feel is hate. I stand and scream at the top of my lungs, anything to vent this rage I feel. After about a minute it passes, and I collapse back to the pillows, exhausted, feeling empty and hopeless.

"Eat," she commands, handing me some fruit. "It's infused with positive energy that will make you feel better."

I managed to get down a strawberry and almost instantly my mood is lifted. A couple more and I'm "right as rain," I hear myself say. She is by my side, holding my hand. He is standing in the corner, looking ashamed and broken.

"That was fucking awful," I mumble.

"That's the dark," he whispers quietly. I've never seen him like this. He looks so broken and afraid.

"There is a catch to what we do," the madam begins to explain. "While I get to feel the benefits of the light when I use it, he has to feel the burn of the dark. We basically feel everything you feel when we pass our powers to you. Good for me, not so much for him. It is also a brutal reminder every time of how he is leaving these poor dolls, and that takes its own toll," she explains.

I almost start to cry again as I look at him in the corner. All those times we violated someone, I assumed he just kept raping them when I left. I had no idea that this was what they were going through. My heart broke for him. No wonder he waited until I left every time—he was trying to protect me. I rise and go to him, letting him wrap his arms around me and bury his head into my shoulder. It's hard to grasp how such a strong man can seem suddenly so vulnerable, how this shared experience has made our bond stronger—light out of dark, I guess.

The madam brings him some fruit and wine. He hungrily consumes it. I can see the energy returning to his body, but his eyes still cry out, barely hiding the pain his soul is forced to bear. I place my hand on his cheek and kiss him.

His embrace around me tightens as he kisses me back. The madam gently rubs our backs. She wants in. We welcome her, and his strong arms envelope both our bodies. We take turns kissing and biting each other's lips and necks. Our passionate exchange brings more life into his tired body. She tears away my robe while dropping hers to the floor; I pull his off his rugged shoulders and let it fall. His engorged cock arouses my desire and I grab it, feeling delight as I slowly start to stroke it. He leans his head back, moaning loudly. It seems he's feeling better. The madam and I kiss his chest, crossing each other as we go, working our way from his muscled pecs down his rock-hard abs. He leans back flat against the wall, gently pulling our hair from our faces so he can watch. We smile at each other. The madam leans in to kiss me, as I stroke his shaft. She is rubbing his balls. His moans get louder. We both focus our attention on his cock, licking the length of it, letting our tongues cross, then taking turns swallowing as much of it as we can. I'm becoming deeply aroused as his tip slides past my lips. I can taste the first of his pre-cum on my tongue. His shaft fills my mouth and I can feel it inching down my throat as I grow braver and take more with each bob of my head. I Look up with satisfaction at the contorted face he is making down at me. I can clearly tell, he is enjoying himself. I let his cock slip out of my mouth and the madam eagerly gobbles it up, not even missing a stroke. She seems to struggle with the girth of it at first, but she is a master and soon I have to pull my hand away as she engulfs his entire length. I hold her hair as she bob's quickly up and down, letting sloppy lines of spittle run down her chin. I squeeze her breasts and she moans a little and works her mouth even harder. She pulls away for a breath, and I resume my position in front of him. I have to brace myself to keep from choking as the madam encourages me forward. He is shaking from excitement and begging me to take more. I close my eyes and let her push my head completely forward until my nose is against his abdomen. I try to roll my tongue around his cock but there is no room, the reflex of my tongue pinned in my mouth and his cock firmly down my throat causes me to gag.

The quick session of my throat muscles tightening shoots pleasure through his body and as I pull away, he mumbles "Oh fuck, I'm so close to cumming!"

We take turns licking the tip and shaft while stroking him, his massive body completely tense, his breath coming in short bursts. It's thrilling to watch how each stroke of my hand and each lap of my tongue brings him closer and closer to climax. My arm tires and she takes hold, swallowing his tip while vigorously stroking him.

"Oh shit!" he stammers, and I see his cock pulsate in her hand, cum bursting from around her lips as he explodes. She pulls away from him to kiss me, forcing my mouth open with her tongue. The warm liquid fills my mouth and spills out, dripping down my chin. She returns her lips to his cock, still stroking it, sucking out every last drop. I swallow my portion of his load quickly, the salty taste lingering on my tongue. I need something sweeter to counter it. She is relaxed in front of him and as she wipes his cum from her breast and lips, I become uncontrollably aroused at the pleasure she seems to take from sucking every last trace from each of her fingers. Slowly placing each one on her tongue then closing her eyes and sucking as she pulls each finger out, taking her time to savor every drop. I look up at him, his jaw is agape, and he is obviously going to be useless for a while. All the better, I want her pussy all to myself. I push her onto her back and before she can react, I have her legs over my shoulders.

"Oh, baby!" she squeals with delight as I pull apart her lips, exposing her to my desperate tongue. Without hesitation, I press my mouth into her. Instantly, I feel her fingers pressing on the back of my head. She likes it, and I want to give her more. I use my tongue to tease her then suck her clit into my mouth, her soft hood played back and forth by my tongue. When she moans, I release my lips and let her clit slip out of my mouth, only to press the width of my tongue against her and let it slide down and back inside her. Her pussy tastes sweet in contrast to his salty cum in my mouth and I hungrily press for more, moving my tongue in every direction until I slide back up to her clit. I work my tongue in every direction I can manage. As her hips begin to gyrate, I match her rhythm, and her grasp on my head tightens. I draw her clit into my mouth again, sucking hard then pressing it back against her, again entering her, wanting to taste more of her in my mouth. My lips as far agape as I can to delve as deep as my physical being will go. She is writhing now, but my tongue is tired. I let my fingers take over, her pelvis pushing into my hand as my two fingers slide easily into her slopping wet pussy and my thumb resumes my tongue's work on her clit. She moans louder, releasing my head and digging her nails into the soft fabric. I can feel my arm tiring and let my tongue loose on her again. I have to hold her down, she is writhing and gyrating so uncontrollably. As her clit disappears behind my lips once more, I feel his strong hands pulling my hips up and spreading me. As he starts to rub my excited cunt, I push back against him. I feel his face on my thighs and then his tongue inside me. His tongue feels nice but it's not what I want.

"Just fuck me, already!" I yell, needing to feel his cock spread me and then fill my insides. I feel the tip of his cock rub against my swollen pussy lips as the dripping juices from my eager box soak his tip. There is a pause for just a second as I pull my face away from her embrace for his penetrating thrust. He bursts into me, Burring the length of his cock all in one long slow confident motion, forcing a rush of adrenaline and pleasure to course through my body from the outside in. The sensation takes my breath away, and I am barely able to keep up with her. My hands take over as an involuntary moan emits from my body. She looks up to see him fucking me. She is obviously pleased and begins toying with herself, watching intently as my body is rocked by his long thrusting motions. I catch my breath and bury my face in her crotch again. The feeling of her on my tongue while he stretches and fills me is overwhelming, but she is getting close. Her moans become long muffled pleas as she bites her lip and drives her fingers harder and faster against herself. I let two of my fingers join my tongue inside her, fighting against the burning in my muscles and the rising tinge of my own building climax!

Her body tenses. I can feel her legs shaking against my face as she rocks wildly to the rhythm of my eager tongue, her pleas for more now just one long "oooh". I hear my own moans, the pleasure of receiving his cock and giving her my tongue is overwhelming my senses

"Don't stop. Oh, don't stop," she cries.

I wouldn't dare, his strong hands pulling hard on my hips as he fucks me harder and harder. With every thrust I feel him slide past my lips, across to the roof of my pussy, filling me until he presses deep inside me. The line between pain and pleasure starts to blur as each thrust feels deeper. I can barely concentrate on the squirming woman my tongue is inside of.

"I'm cumming, I'm cumming!" she cries out, over and over.

Her whole body goes rigid. I bury my fingers inside her, pushing past her clenching muscles, and she cries out more. It's everything I can do to stay inside her as she shakes and pulls at me, her lady juice gushing around my fingers and down my wrist. My own excitement grows as I watch her body convulse in the grip of the orgasm and even as it begins to wane, every twitch of my fingers seems to send her back over the edge. Her satisfied pussy releases its grip on my fingers, and I drop to my elbows, focusing entirely on his cock ravaging my hole.

The sensation of his rhythmic pounding consumes my whole body and I feel like I am floating at the edge of a waterfall, getting closer to the crest, each thrust a wave moving me toward a cascade of ecstasy.

I feel her hands moving down my back, soft and slow. The erotic feeling of her hands tracing across my body gives me renewed excitement and as her hands spread my cheeks, I feel the need for her to penetrate me. I hear myself begging for it.

"Please, please, please," over and over. The waterfall is close, the waves pushing me towards the edge. It keeps getting bigger and bigger, the long-awaited warmth pushing out from deep inside.

Her fingers slide along my petals, teasing the edges of his cock. I can hear his familiar moans, building up to his own climax. I want it. I want him to cum inside me while I'm cumming. I want to yell it, but all I can get out is "Make me cum, make me cum. Please, make me cum."

She smacks my ass with one hand while forcing two fingers into me beside his cock. The sudden increase in pressure makes us both cry out. She withdraws one finger, tracing it around my dark hole, teasing me and slicking my hole with my own wetness. I am so close, the forbidden sensation electrifying the nerves in my entire body. My breath shortens, and I slam back hard against his cock, craving his penetrating force deep inside me. I know he's close, his movements systematic and rigid as he tries to use all his self-control to fuck me. The madam doesn't hesitate and punches her finger into my quivering darkness. Her two tiny fingers impossibly deep in me as the shock of the new and overwhelming sensation pushes us both to cum—him in great hot bursts, shooting inside me and gushing out along his cock as he continues to pump new loads into me, mine like an explosion, so long in building now coursing out to every cell in my body, wiping every other sensation but this ecstasy away and leaving a crashing wave of satisfaction washing over me, until even my toes feel complete!

I fall forward, spent, my body still quivering, glistening with sweat. I want to speak, but I'm breathless. I stretch out flat. Relaxed, satisfied.

He crashes down beside me. Through breathless lips he just keeps muttering, "Wow."

"Three for three, a job well done then."

The madam's voice breaks the silence as she lays her body to the other side of mine, in what is becoming a familiar and elegant fashion. For a moment, we just enjoy the silence and the light touch of our bodies lying so close together. I feel sleep falling upon me and as I struggle to keep my eyes open the madam claps twice, and the funny little man appears. This time, he is carrying a tray of chocolates and a container of semi-clear liquid. Starting with the madam, he feeds us each a chocolate and then pours a glass of this new beverage. To my surprise, it is cold. Yet another luxury that is rare to come across in the dusty world below. The rich chocolate flavor ignites with a sip of this drink and as the cool liquid slides down my throat and the chocolate melts on my tongue, a feeling of calm and peace passes over me. I am expecting the same energetic burst I had received from the fruit earlier, but this is different. I still feel lifted inside, but instead of being invigorated I am overcome with a sense of calm, even euphoria. I soon find myself feeling totally carefree. Even the pillow feels softer. Like I am in a weightless cloud, and millions of soft feathers are gently brushing over me followed by kisses from the softest of lips. I managed to casually glance to my side and see both the madam and my lover are given to a similar state. The little man is not so fortunate and is working diligently to gently scrub every inch of the madam's body, an act that seems peculiar until he gets to mine.

As he wets the cloth and runs it over my body, it leaves a gleaming trail of soothing warmth that feels like it is soaking into my skin and loosening every muscle and joint down to the bone. The little man works efficiently, moving from my legs quickly to my arms. I feel limp, relaxed, and clean. My torso is no different and the gentle touch of his hands lull me into a helpless state. He finishes by placing a mask on my face that makes my skin tingle and my mind go blank. I close my eyes and am only vaguely aware of his presence as he passes a brush through my hair gently pulling years of tangles and tension from my scalp and letting me slip peacefully into a deep sleep.

 As I drift off, I am only barely aware of a voice in the back of my mind saying, "What happens when you wake up?" To be honest, I really don't care, and for the first time in years I fell into a deep slumber, totally at peace.

The dream is brief but foreboding. I am running down a long dark hallway, naked. Pulling me along with him is my lover, his body not yet scarred but his skin bloody. I remember this tunnel. I remember this exact moment—It was when we escaped from the governor. Only this time, I have turned to look back. I was too scared to before, but in this dream, I have to. I see what appears to be the governor pulling in a cloud of green light around him. As the cloud grows, the people in the circle drop, but when they hit the ground they turn to nothing, just dust that blows away. I see the governor's face, twisted and angry. He throws his arms down and yells and a great ball of green fire shoots toward us. I want to look away, but I can't. Even as I feel the heat on my face, I can't turn away. Finally, as I feel the flame lick my bare skin, I am able to close my eyes and scream!

I awake, startled and a little confused. As my hands pass over my skin to check for burns, the reality that it was just a dream creeps in. Unsettled, I try to calm myself. It is then that I remember my surroundings. Where I lay in the middle of the room is dark, but as I stand, lights above me slowly became brighter, allowing my eyes to adjust. The little man is obediently kneeling in front of me, in his outstretched hand another silver tray of food. I thank him, and as he sets the tray down and disappears in his usual fashion I look around for my companions. They are at the far end of the room, fully dressed, standing in front of the screens. On two of the screens are maps with several points marked out, meaningless lines and numbers drawn around them. I recognize the maps. I have the same ones stashed away on my bike. They are maps of Wasteland with all the major towns labeled, including the capitol where the governor lives, locked away in his cave. A shudder passes over me as I recall the dream, but it quickly passes. On the third screen are pictures of faces with some kind of profile written next to them. The pictures flip through quickly, and I notice that many have a large X through them. A lot of the faces look familiar—In fact, some I even killed myself. All of them were the governor's henchman. On the last screen, it looks like a video of a group of people sitting in a semicircle at a large table, facing the screen from the other side. It is then I notice my companions talking to the screen, and after a second, I realize the screen is talking back.

"Of course," I mumble to myself, "magic food, mind blowing sex, a weird pervy servant in spandex with a boner—why not have talking screens."

I sit and watch them, bemused as the conversation gets quite heated. Stern words are whispered loudly, I assume for my benefit, and then with a final say, the people on the other side of the screen end the conversation and the two grow silent. There is some formal saluting and then the screen goes blank. They turn to each other and continue to talk quietly, but it was obvious they are having an argument. Out of nowhere, a memory of my parents arguing the same way crops up. My parents were arguing about something I broke and whether or not I should be punished. A funny little memory to have now, it just all seems so familiar. It is then that I realized the two are arguing about me and perhaps I should join them. Is also then that I notice I am still naked. My companions, however, are neatly dressed. It strikes me, the contrast, that is. With the two of them dressed and me standing here naked, I feel oddly vulnerable. Silly, considering the night we just shared. I feel in no way embarrassed or even really the need to cover myself. If anything, I am secretly hoping they will see I am awake and choose to strip and join me. It is not to be, however, so I sit calmly on the couch and wait for my companions to invite me over. As I watch them argue, I can't help but notice the outfits they are wearing are new and quite different from the ones they arrived in. He is clad in his typical leather, only now he has thick armor pads buckled and belted in strategic locations across his chest and back. Multiple weapons in pouches and tools are strapped anywhere they can be without impeding his movement. His heavy boots make him stand even taller and more intimidating than his usual giant frame exudes. She can't be more the opposite—where he is a good foot taller than me, she is at least four inches shorter. Her petite frame looks frail next to his muscular build, her frilly blue skirt and tiny halter top doing little to hide her feminine attributes. In fact, it seems that while he covers everything in armor and weapons, she is going to great lengths to show as much of her well-toned body as possible. Her skirt, while long in the back, is extremely short in the front—so short that there is a hope that a little breeze or uncalculated movement might reveal the miniscule panties she wears underneath. The only real protection for her legs is a pair of knee-high boots with surprisingly high heels that make her just a little taller than me. Escaping from the tops of her boots, black nylons securely held in place by the garter straps stop mid-thigh, leaving smooth silky skin exposed to the elements and the relentless gaze of everyone she passes. Of course, her thighs are not all that is exposed. The madam is of course acutely aware of the power she holds over people with her perfect physique, a power she wields expertly to her advantage. The top of her skirt stops abruptly at her hips, held fast with a wide black leather belt that seems to hug her just tight enough to keep the fabric it holds from slipping away, leaving her completely bare. Oh, how I want to pull that belt away. Such a simple leather band must be purely for decoration as there is not so much as a sharp edge on it. Secretly, I am hopeful she has a better weapon hidden somewhere because the belt will be useless for self-defense.

The distance from her belt to her top is considerable and as my eye follows her bare skin from the curve of her hips, past her taught stomach, my gaze is distracted just short of seeing her ample bosom, practically bursting out from behind the thin strip of blue fabric that seems to magically hold her breasts tight, even push them out a little at the top. It seems like a miracle of textile engineering to me. Aside from the strip around her bosom, just one piece of fabric over her shoulder seems to be all that is keeping her covered enough to be able to walk down the street without causing a full-blown riot. Although I can recall hearing stories about her causing riots fully dressed, so I guess it doesn't matter if that little strap holds firm or not. Her beauty is definitely her finest weapon. As I sit gazing at the two of them, I realize I have become quite aroused, and the more I think about the previous evening the wetter I get. Before I can go to town on myself, however, the little man reappears. In his arms he is holding my clothes, freshly washed and folded. Again, I thank him, but before he can leave, I stop him.

"So, what's your deal? Why the spandex and boner all the time?" I ask.

He looks around nervously and in a quiet voice responds. "I'm not really supposed to talk without permission."

I lean forward, putting my breast eye level with him. "Can't I give you permission? Aren't I special enough?"

His eyes are transfixed on my hard nipples, so I lean in further.

"Of course, you are," he said, after way too many seconds pass in silence. "It's just a little embarrassing, that's all."

"You gave me a sponge bath last night and just almost caught me masturbating. I think we're past a little embarrassing."

Upon hearing me mention masturbation, his face gets red and then he speaks.

"I wear this, and I'm stuck with this," he said, pointing to his clothes and boner respectively, "because I am a criminal. I was caught watching some girls in the shower and so I got sentenced to two years as a Gimp servant."

"Two things—first, two years for peeping? And second, what is a Gimp servant?" I ask.

He replies, "Well, it was like one hundred women...and I made recordings...and I may have sold them...a lot."

"Wow, okay then. That makes sense, and the Gimp part?" I ask

"The Gimp part is the punishment of humiliation. When you're sentenced, they give you a medicine that gives you a permanent erection, but you can never climax. The suit is actually a special fabric that is both itchy and also very erotic adding to your misery and frustration. The servant part is to repay your debt to the people you wronged. Gimps are assigned as servants and depending on the severity of your crime, dictates the severity that your master's can punish you. I only watched, so masters can't physically do anything to me, but they can make me watch or perform anything they say as long as I don't have to touch them."

"But the baths last night?"

"Well, I don't have to, but these particular masters are risking their lives to save all of us. So, cleaning them up, an occasional massage, or even helping in a sexual tryst once in a while seems like the least, I can do. Plus, they're both super fucking hot!" And with that, he quickly scurried away.

I can't help but smile as I watch his funny little walk and that spandex ride up his little butt crack. *"What a silly little goofball."* Two years for peeping. Hell, in Wasteland he would have been ridiculed for only peeping. Even the little kids would probably beat him up.

As I dress, I realize what a busy little bee my new pervy friend has been. My skirt and bustle are modified. The fabric has been replaced with the same silken fabric as the madam's, only in black. As I run it through my fingers, I can feel that there is a much higher quality to it. It's obviously not from around here. There are flowing layers in the back arched by a new bustle made out of a very light and—I realize as I try to bend it—strong material. As I inspect it further, I realize he has built in several more holsters as well as lightweight armor along the interior. The front is bundled short like the madam's, but I discover in the belt a switch that drops it to full length and lo and behold more armor! To my surprise, I find something else hidden in this belt—two twelve-inch daggers whose blades curve with the belt but slice like a rigid blade, even stab when twisted correctly. My boots are upgraded as well. I inspect the length of them and realize they are armor plated and the six-inch platform heels hide so much more.

The platform is modified with some sort of spring system to make me able to run and jump way higher than I ever could before. There is also another holster built into the back of them. The Super skimpy shorts that have replaced my trusty old leather ones are actually some sort of crazy material. There is padding in the seat, and a lining that can cool me, as well as multiple layers at work to control moisture so I never sweat, and holy crap are they comfortable, all while looking like I'm wearing practically nothing.

"Really flatters the form," I catch myself saying as I look back at how hot my ass looks. Impressive yes, but the best is yet to come. I slip on my corset to find it is changed quite a lot as well. As I slide it into place it tightens automatically, squeezing my frame snugly and pushing my ample bosom up. "A little more cleavage than I usually rock, but that's all good."

I look over my well-fitted garment to discover it has also been modified for protection and usability, as well as looks. Hidden weapons, secret pockets. I half expect my shoulder armor to shoot flames. Shit, on second thought it might. I should be careful. The two see me dressing and beckon me over. I greet both of them with a smile as I take my first awkward steps in my new super boots. By the fourth step I have it and by the fifth my strut is on point. I can tell I'm rocking it, the way they're both staring at me as I walk toward them.

The madam approaches me, inspecting my outfit, running her hands over the buckles and fabric. It feels so good to have her touching me. Thank God these panties control moisture.

"Damn girl, that little freak is a hell of a seamstress," my lover touts, unable to take his eyes off me. I play it cool, but inside I'm glowing. I have always tried to keep a low profile, go unnoticed, but the attention I'm getting is marvelous and I can't help but to enjoy it.

"Eyes up here, buddy," I tease as I catch his gaze lingering a little too long at the top of my corset.

"As much as I want to rip all of this off of you, and I most definitely will later, we should probably go over the plan."

The madam's tone has changed from flirty to serious and I realize that all of this isn't to keep me from getting scrapes on my motorcycle. It has a singular purpose. Bring down the governor.

"The plan is simple," she starts, "we need to boost your light energy, get you to seduce one of the governor's goons. Then we let him take you long enough that the governor will be able to track your scent. You let yourself get captured and taken to the governor and then you use your dark energy to destroy him and then escape."

"Okay, well that makes sense—a bit lite on the details but, you know, definitely easy to remember."

My sarcasm does not seem to be appreciated.

"Obviously, there is a lot of prep we have to do." He speaks in an unfamiliar serious tone. "First things first, we're going to have to train you how to switch your power back and forth. Between the two of us we can give you enough dark power to kill him and enough light to mask it. You will have to be able to switch at the last second when it's too late to break his connection with you, and he will be forced to absorb the dark."

"Okay, that sounds intense."

"It is," she replies, "and it gets worse. Last night you had just a tiny amount of dark energy transferred to you. The amount we're talking about is at least one hundred times that. I'll be able to transfer light while he transfers dark into you so you won't be affected too badly by the initial transfer, but no one will be there to help you when you transfer it to the governor. You will see all his darkest secrets, know his pain, experience all of his fears, and it will be unbelievably intense. The actual energy transfer will last less than a minute, but it will feel like days, possibly even weeks. No one knows. A transfer like this has never been successfully tried."

"Oh good, so I might go crazy, and kill myself or just plain explode?"

"You probably won't explode," he chimes in, obviously missing the sarcasm again!

"So, what's the biggest transfer that's been done? How far into new ground are we trending here?" I ask

She speaks, "About one-tenth what we want to give you, and no, the subject did not survive."

A silent pall falls over the room.

"Do I want to know how they died?"

"Quickly, if that helps," he adds.

It doesn't.

"I don't understand what makes you think I can do this. I'm just a Raider. I've survived by killing out of necessity, not pleasure. I have a horrible temper, I have no special gifts or powers. What makes me different than the poor fool that got blown up before?"

I can feel tears forming again. What the fuck? Twice in two days. This emotion shit is ridiculous. The madam touches my arm lightly.

"When your lover first found you, he saw through the light to the darkness that was growing inside you. That's why he saved you. He knew when the governor got to you, he would see it and kill you instantly, wasting an opportunity for us to destroy him. Originally, your lover was the one that was supposed to use his dark energy to kill the governor, but the governor sensed it in him and captured him, then made him watch as he killed hundreds right in front of him before he finally was able to break free the night you were brought in. The darkness you had that day grew, as well as your light energy. Somehow, you were becoming more powerful on your own. By the time you rescued me you were already more powerful then all of his henchmen. And you did it on your own, without knowing. Think about all the things you can do, almost without even trying. Sniper shots from over a mile away in almost complete darkness. Nearly inexhaustible strength, hell even learning to swim in a matter of seconds. Normal people can't do any of that."

The madam is on her knees in front of me, practically begging me to believe her and listen.

"I brought you here to use you, but then we went swimming. I was just trying to calm you, get you to trust me so I could ask for your help, but as we kissed and with every touch, I could see the darkness leave you. Then on the beach, I didn't mean to give you the light, you took it. I don't know how. It should not have been possible, but you absorbed my light energy and it wiped out all your dark energy. That's why we think you can do this, and more importantly that's why we think you can survive this and walk out of that cave as the hero of Wasteland!"

I don't want to believe her. I search her face for any sign of deception. Instead, I find myself locked into her gaze, the sadness in her eyes cutting through my soul. It doesn't make sense, any of it. My mind is screaming run, but I can't. Even if it's total bullshit, my goal all along is to kill the governor, so I guess I'm in, even if it kills me.

"All right, fine, I'm in. I gave you my word earlier and I will stick to it, but you have to promise me one thing."

"Anything." She smiles back.

"Before I go down there, I want another one of your starlight magic pussy eating orgasms!"

She laughs. "Baby, I'll give you two and even have him throw a couple your way!"

"It's settled then, let's get back to the plan." I sigh as I accept my inevitable fate. Everyone dies, I think to myself, at least I get to go out with a bang! I hear the heavy locks slide into place as the large door closes and the training begins.

Chapter 6

Revenge is at Hand

As we head down the trail, I relish the last of the bright sunshine and clear skies before we are swallowed by the dust. We've been locked in that mountain for two months, and as the warm air rushes past my skin I am reminded of the sense of pure freedom I use to feel, tearing across the barren and dusty plains of the Wasteland. A sense of serious urgency has come over our little group. We received word that the governor is collecting his next batch of dolls and the decision was made that I should be in that batch. I look over at my two companions. His large muscular body seems to dwarf the motorcycle as well as his passenger on the back. Her long skirts flow freely out behind her, like a peacock's tail—colorful and intoxicating, but as I now know incredibly deadly. My own thoughts fill my mind. Despite the possible consequences, a rare sense of hope fills me. All these years, all this suffering, could be over in a matter of days. I catch myself letting my mind drift to what my world might be like once this is all over if, that is, I survive.

My focus returns as we enter the dust. The enveloping cloud of hot gritty air hits me like a blast in the face. My new outfit protects most of my body, but a small portion of my face is exposed between my scarf and goggles. The sting of the sand against my cheek brings with it the old feelings of foreboding and the fear of the unknown.

We reach the bottom of the mountain and pick up speed. Our race to get to the little town we've chosen before the governor's goons is on, and for the first time in my life I feel as though time is slipping away from me instead of lingering on forever. Soon enough, however, I can see the gates looming in the distance. My companions split off. We need to arrive separately to not arouse suspicion. Traders are common at towns like this, but three heavily armed people arriving at the same time will definitely be noticed by the wrong people. I pull off on a bluff overlooking the town. With my new goggles I can zoom in and watch my friends enter the gates. At first, there is some resistance to their arrival. My lover seems to be having a bit of trouble coming across as just a friendly trader. The madam dismounts from the bike and removes the poncho she was wearing to protect herself from the brutal ride. At the first sight of her, the gates are thrown open and the two are welcomed in. The madam lets the gate keeper lead her in by the hand as a swarm of men fall in behind her. For a second it looks like they are going to have a parade in her honor with the horde of people following her down the street. I can't help but laugh to myself how easily these men fall under her spell. I scan back to the now unguarded gate. My lover slips quietly through and down a side street. No parade for him. Just as well. He never does well in crowds.

I make myself comfortable as I wait for dusk. Once the madam has all the men in town good and drunk it will be safe for me to join her at the saloon, but for now I just have to wait. I try to stay focused, but my mind continues to drift back to the hard days and bliss-filled nights on top of the mountain. I can't tell if it's my nerves or if I really am feeling sentimental, but I find myself letting my fingers run across my body thinking of the way she touched me. How strong his arms felt around me, the soft kisses she would give me randomly. "Just because," she would say. I miss them both already and like a fool let my imagination dream of a time when we could all be together again. My daydreams are interrupted by the first shadows of dusk falling across the land. It's time. I collect my thoughts and hop on my bike. With a twist of the throttle I head toward my destiny.

I slow to a crawl as I ride through the gates. Watchful eyes cautiously measure me up and down as I roll through the streets toward the center of town. It's hard not to be unnerved by the faces appearing in the windows, summing me up then retreating back into the dark. The buildings are full, but the streets are nearly deserted. Bad news travels fast here and the governor's henchmen on the prowl seems to have put everyone on edge. I head for the saloon, throwing off my own cloak and letting my bare skin feel the night air. I am hopeful that the sight of my bare flesh and female form will throw the governor's spies off their game. Might as well let myself be seen. After all, bait only works if you can attract your prey's attention. I wind through the dusty streets until I pull up in front of the saloon. I can see several shapes moving inside, but none seem to pay much attention to me as I dismount and secure my gear. I take a deep breath and walk through the doors. I pull away my goggles and scarf. The room is oddly cheerful. The whole place seems to be alight with cheerful music and even some dancing. No surprise, the madam is perched on the piano leading a group in a drunken sing-along of some sort. Drinks are flowing all around. I do my best not to make eye contact as I walk past her to the bar.

"Cup of the Brown," I order as confidently as I can muster. I am doing my best to stay calm, but my nerves are rattled. Just knowing what's in store and what is at stake has me shaking. What if I can't get the attention of one of his men? I am past the usual age of most of his victims, after all. Or worse, what if I give myself away and get us all killed. The thought of failing my companions shakes me to my core and I regain my composure.

The bartender obliges, pouring my drink without so much as a second glance. He is entranced by the scantily clad woman on the piano and if I'm honest, I can't blame him. I turn my back to the bar to watch the show. The madam's breasts bounce gingerly as she claps along to the music. The group around her continues to grow and the men have taken to dancing with each other, some sort of proxy for the beauty perched on full display in front of them. No one seems to have a care in the world as long as the music is good and the whiskey flows. All attention remains on the now dancing madam as she works her way across the room, luring more hapless fools with her seductive moves. Her skirt twirls and flutters in the air as she spins teasing the poor fools with quick glimpses of her thighs and panties as she glides across the floor. She reaches me and stops for a kiss, running her hand up my leg and teasing between my thighs. Stealing my scarf to expose more of my breasts, she turns to face the drooling group of despots behind her.

"If you had tits like this, I'd kiss you too!" she remarks coyly to her fans as they hoot and howl.

The crowd moves on, but now I can feel several sets of eyes on me. I do my best to show off my assets— leaning against the bar, letting my skirt fall away, exposing bare my legs, even deep breaths to make my bosom heave seductively. From a dark corner a large man approaches, his hat pulled low over his eyes. He looks up and catches my gaze. I'm caught off guard by his piercing blue eyes and a squared jaw. The sort of strong features I find myself undeniably attracted to. He reaches out his hand to ask for a dance and I find myself compelled to accept ,reaching out and taking his hand, letting him lead me to the middle of the floor. His body presses tight to mine. We move surprisingly gracefully around the dance floor. I didn't even know I could dance. Even more surprising is that I am actually enjoying the moment. I let myself go and find my rhythm in step with his as we cascade across the floor, the piano player crudely banging away in the background, setting the rhythm to our steps. When the song ends, I lead him back to the bar, doing my best to look memorized by his eyes, and more than a little turned on by the strength in his arms as he pressed me tight against his chest while we danced. He orders us both a drink. The bartender hurriedly fills the glasses and sheepishly backs away.

"Apparently you have some clout in this town," I say, nodding at the retreating bartender.

"Well, I'm good at keeping things peaceful around here," he replies, trying to nonchalantly let his badge show from behind his jacket. His dry gravelly voice awakens an undeniable heat in my loins.

"Well, officer, perhaps you can tell me why the streets are so quiet, but this place is roaring like a party?" I ask as I lean into his arms, causing him to look down to meet my gaze and of course notice my breasts as I try my best to flaunt them. He smiles as he shifts his position for a better view, letting his hand fall gently to the top of my knee. I place my hand over his and slowly pull it up towards my exposed flesh. His eyes widen as his fingers reach the soft skin of my thigh above my boot and I can see his guard falling away as his sizable erection grows. I have to be careful. I am dripping wet at this point and one wrong move will turn my quest for information into a hardcore fuck fest really fast. Luckily, he seems to be less guarded with his information and as he strokes my thighs, he spills his guts.

"Someone spotted a couple of the governor's men next town over. Apparently, they are out looking for fresh meat. Folks around here just as soon not risk it and stay out of site till the threats pass."

"Not you, though?" I quiz him.

"I've got nothing they want, although you might want to find a place to be scarce. Pretty thing like yourself might be too much for these animals to resist. You know they rent rooms upstairs. I would be happy to keep you safe until they are gone if you want the company."

Too easy, I think to myself. And with my best coy smile and a kiss on the cheek I reply, "Why don't you get us a key?"

Without looking away from me, he motions the bartender again. This time the man produces a brass key and places it in my new acquaintances hand. With a broad smile exposing a perfect set of bright white teeth, the sheriff takes my hand.

"Shall we?"

"Indeed!" I eagerly reply.

There might be a chance to mix business with pleasure yet, I think to myself. As we pass through the bar and head up the creaky wooden staircase, I catch the madam, nodding with concerned approval as she watches our ascent. Of all the psycho dirt bag undercover agents at the governor's disposal I definitely picked the most attractive one. Thank God for that.

"I hope you won't just be protecting me," I whisper into his ear as the key slips into the lock.

"I'm sure I can think of a few ways to keep you entertained," he whispers back.

The key turns, freeing the handle from its catch and letting the door swing wide open. I gracefully enter the room first. allowing him to close and lock the door behind us. With one stride he's behind me, his strong hands encompassing my shoulders and his hot breath on my neck.

"You don't waste anytime," I coo.

"Shut the fuck up, bitch!" he barks, pushing me down on my stomach on the bed. That didn't take long. *So much for not getting one of the rapey ones,* I think to myself, as he fights with the buckles and straps holding my corset in place. I carefully release my belt before he flips me over, tearing my corset away. In my mind, I know this is part of the plan, but I am having trouble not snapping this pricks neck. I have to keep reminding myself why I am here. Motivation to play my part as the victim. I try to struggle to free myself, but he takes both my hands in his one massive paw and pins them above my head. Pulling away my skirt and shorts, he leaves me completely exposed, naked on the bed with just my choker and thigh high boots remaining undisturbed. Part of me wants to scream. I spent my life not letting myself be a victim, not since the first time, yet here I am, practically offering it to this disgusting pig. He slaps me, and uses his belt to tie my hands to the headboard. I squirm to try to free myself, to no avail. The thought pops into my head that this may have gotten a little out of hand.

 It's painfully obvious that he's done this before. Once he has me secured, he stands back, quite pleased with himself, laughing at his own handiwork.

"Well, you're just too good to be true. I guess the governor is going to have to settle for one less dirty little slut because I'm going to fuck you to death!"

I spit in his face and try to kick him. He pins my legs with his knees.

"Now, now, don't be such a little cunt. Believe me when I say I can make this so much worse!"

My legs burn as his knees dig into them. I am still struggling, trying to free myself. My mind starts to race. An unfamiliar feeling of panic creeps up my spine. My whole body is suddenly tense at the feel of his giant tongue on my body. He starts at my breast, licking and slobbering as he goes. He feels more like a reptile tasting its next meal than a man.

"I can taste the fear on you!" He happily retorts as his tongue sloppily licks its way to my belly button.

The panic is real now. I can feel the tears running down my cheeks. I cry out for help. He just laughs louder.

"You stupid little whore, who the fuck do you think is going to help you?"

The door bursts open, and my two companions storm in. I can tell from his silence he is beyond confused, not to mention blown away at the audacity of these two interlopers bursting into *HIS* room.

"What the shit? Do you know who the fuck you're barging in on?" he finally stammers out.

A swift blow to the face by my lover, and he hits the floor. The madam unties me and without thinking I run over and kick him in the balls, twice. He howls in pain. It's music to my ears.

"Naughty, naughty, boy," my lover angrily scolds him as he pulls him up by his hair, only to beat him down again. The sounds of the bones breaking in the man's face is a pleasant ring in my ears.

"Remember, unconscious, not dead!" the madam reminds him. "We don't want to have to do this again."

I feel the warm glow of her energy passing to me through her gentle touch. She kisses me, gently wiping the tears away with her hand.

"You sure he will smell her on him?" my lover asks, standing over the man and seething with hate, wanting to make him suffer more for what he has done to me.

"He tasted her sweat. That evil cock sucker will be on her scent the second he walks in the room," she replies, returning her attention to help me dress.

"What if he talks?" he asks.

"It won't matter. The governor won't believe him even if he does tell the truth. He'll probably just kill him on sight for trying to steal such a prize from him. Better than what this prick deserves, if I'm honest!" she assures me.

"Well, better safe than sorry," my lover chimes in, unable to resist the urge to cause the sheriff further harm.

A few more strong blows and my attacker is in a bloody lump on the floor. I can see that his jaw is clearly broken in several places as it hangs limp from his pulpy face. His shallow ratcheting breath sounds wet and labored. My lover looks rather pleased with himself as he pulls a red-hot poker from the fire.

"I learned some things about our noble sheriff here while I've been scouting out this town. It seems only fair we show him the gracious hospitality he has shown all the other little girls he's brought to this room."

Barely conscious, the man sees the poker and tries to crawl away, whimpering in fear and pain. It does nothing to deter my lover. If anything, it seems to encourage him. He kicks the man's legs open and with one powerful stroke shoves the poker deep into his rectum. The cries of pain and the smell of burning flesh fill the room and flood our senses. My strong urge to finish the job and rip his testicles off is dissuaded by the pleasure I get from watching him suffer. This is, after all, the closest thing to justice you can get in Wasteland. Part of me is hoping I will get the chance to tear him apart somewhere in the future, even though I know it's doubtful. This swine's life span can be measured in hours now. The damage from his injuries will lead to a slow agonizing death before the next sunrise. Shame, I still feel like it should take much longer.

I walk over and stand in front of the whimpering naked body on the floor. *"Pathetic,"* I whisper to myself, and with a swift kick to the face I put him out.

We quietly leave the room and then the bar. It seems my companions made quite the mess coming to my rescue. The saloon is empty save for the six or seven bodies on the floor, and the complacent bartender slumped over his bar. All well-deserved, I imagine. We round the corner and enter a small house down the street. The family is gone. Run out by my companion—an act of terror that in all actuality is an act of mercy. Things will get ugly when the governor finds the bodies in the saloon. We clear a spot in the middle of the floor and they each take one of my hands.

"Are you ready?" the madam asks.

I nod, reluctantly.

"Okay. Let's do this."

I close my eyes and feel their power rushing in from both sides, the light spinning against the dark. A torrent fills my body. So much good, so much evil, my mind is completely chaotic. Jumping from good memories to bad, emotions rushing through me so fast I can barely keep up with them. I keep trying to focus on my one positive thought, the way they trained me to do, but as the transfer continues, I feel it slipping away. It's so much, I can feel it pulling at me, like my entire being is getting penetrated by bolts of lightning and furious lashes from a flaming whip. I feel their grips tighten as I start to lose consciousness. I can barely hear the madam, her voice softly encouraging me. The pain is so great, I'm holding on with all my will, and then just before I black out, I hear him blurt out.

"There, that's all of it! We're done!"

As they drop my hand, I go limp. A fully charged weapon, pathetically passed out on the floor, totally useless.

It's night when I wake. My head rests comfortably in the lap of the madam as she runs her fingers through my hair, her soft touch bringing life back to me one gentle stroke at a time. She is looking into my eyes as I open them, and I can see the pain in her soul. She leans down to kiss me—no spark this time, just a passionate kiss between two lovers. Her soft lips are warm and wet against mine, her sweet essence a refreshing change from the taste of burning ash and metal the transfer left in my mouth. No words are spoken. None need to be. Everything that we need to say has already been said. Now we're just laying here in silence enjoying our last minutes of peace together before he finds me. My fear is gone. As the seconds roll past, I feel stronger and stronger. Still, though, I lie in her embrace, greedily coveting every second I have with her arms around me. She has given me her body, her soul, and her power, and now with the last of her strength she is giving me comfort and love, the only thing she has left to give.

There is a loud commotion in the street. I start to sit upright, but she stops me.

"He's here," she whispers, weakly fighting back tears.

Apparently, we went a bit overboard with our little ploy to get his attention. I can hear from the commotion on the street that there must be at least thirty men outside looking for us. I guess our plan worked a bit too well. The governor never leaves the cave, but now he's here, walking the streets!

"What do we do? Can your people use the machine to get him?" I ask.

"I don't know," she cries. "The governor has made all communication with them impossible. His energy is blocking our transmissions. We can only hope they are watching and see us here."

"We stick to the plan." My lover appears from the darkness. At first, I am appalled he doesn't want to fight, that he is willing to just give up, until I see him in the light. His eyes sunken, his skin pale. His whole body appears withdrawn, withered, and tired. I turn to the madam for confirmation. The dim light through the window reveals she is in a similar physical state.

"There must be a way for the two of you to still escape!" I plead with them.

"He's right, it's our best option. We can't risk this plan failing."

"I don't understand. You two are supposed to escape so we can meet up at the lake after..." My words trail off as I realize the awful truth that they have been hiding from me. For them there is no escape. They are already dead.

Her words are muddled as she fights back tears. At first, it seems that she is crying from fear—fear for her safety, fear for mine, fear that our plan will fail. I've put it together too late. As my lover helps her to her feet, I realize it's not fear, it's pain. My two companions literally have given me everything. All the power they had stored up for this plus their remaining life force. They are dying, slowly disintegrating from the inside out. They help each other across the room and as I realize I will never see them again I reach out, wanting to cry out, to run to them and embrace them one last time. I do nothing—just sit in a pathetic sobbing pile on the floor, tears streaming down my cheeks, as they open the door. They both look back at me and smile as their bodies finally fail them and they collapse into dust, instantly blown away by the never ceasing wind. I continue to cry. I let my sobs turn into howls, holding my knees to my chest, burying my head in my skirt. I cry, even as I hear the front door shatter and heavy footsteps approach. My mind is screaming at me. Stick to the plan. Don't make their sacrifice in vain. My hands trace the triggers of my pistols, and the rage that fills me is all consuming. I want to kill them all, but I know I would never be able to get to the governor with just bullets. I feel helpless and emotionally destroyed, so I just sit in the middle of the floor and play my part as the helpless victim. I know this is the part of the plan where I am supposed to be taken. No point in fighting it. I suppress the urge to fight, to make all of his men pay for making my friends suffer, and I just weep.

Chapter 7

Taken

I can feel people standing around me, hear their voices. I want them to go away, just let me mourn the loss of my friends for a few more minutes. I know they won't. I know I'm going with them; I know it's my chance to kill the governor.

I can hear low voices through my sobs, indistinguishable from one to the next. I hear them discussing my fate.

"So, this is the little bitch you saw him take upstairs?"

"Yeah, that's her."

"We should shove a fucking poker through her god damned head!"

"Are you fucking nuts? The gov wants this one intact, and if you think a poker up the ass is bad just think what that sadistic fuck will do if he finds out you fucked this up!"

"It's not right. No respect for the law! None! It's not right, I'm telling ya!"

"Would you two shut the fuck up? For Gods' sakes, just pick her up and bring her out. It's time she got to meet the governor."

I feel rough hands grab my arms and as the two men lift me to my feet I don't resist. I just stay limp in their arms, making them drag me out. I'm thrown to my knees in the middle of the dusty street. I am bemused by the naked and beaten body of my would-be attacker next to me, the poker still firmly planted in his ass with just the handle showing. I can't help but to smile a little at the absurdity of it. My former lover definitely had a twisted sense of humor. The body trembles and I realize he is still alive. I can't resist. I lean down and whisper in his swollen bloody ear as I twist the poker deeper into him.

"How'd that work out for ya, you fucktard!"

There is a swift kick to my ribs. Apparently, I upset one of his loyal law-abiding minions.

"You leave him alone, you psycho bitch!" he passionately yells at me.

A shot rings out, and the minion drops. A trickle of blood oozes from the hole between his eyes.

"No one is to disrespect the governor's wishes, and the governor wants this one alive and unharmed!"

I look up and see a massive man standing over me, smoke still escaping from the barrel of his pistol. His face seems timeless. I can't tell if he's twenty or two hundred. Somehow, both seem possible. His massive frame looks to be made of stone, the leather binding his flesh is stretched tight, revealing every rippling muscle. It's his eyes that cut into me. Dark black eyes with no soul. I have seen these eyes before. It's the governor. He leans down, bringing his face close to mine, and a wicked smile reveals his rows of jagged white teeth—sharp points in his mouth like a cage of daggers to hold back his black tongue. He inspects the writhing body of the man next to me. He seems unimpressed.

"That's how we found him sir. We're sure she did it. He is a loyal man to you sir; we were hoping you could fix him up…. sir." The pathetic voice behind me seems terrified to even be addressing him.

The large man leans down, sniffing the air.

"This man has gone where he was told not to go. His sentence is death."

I guess I am glad to know our plan would have worked even if these goons hadn't found me so fast. The madam was right about him sniffing me out.

The large man picks up the withered sheriff by his head, letting his feet dangle as he looks into his eyes one last time before quickly jerking his arm, snapping the man's neck clean. He drops him to the ground as if he were disposing of an empty bottle and turns to the other two.

"Take her to the cave, and make sure nothing happens to her or I'll peel your skin and leave you for the ants to finish." He kneels down and lifts my head to meet his stare. "Time to go meet the boss."

I thought he was the boss! I'm confused by his last statement, but before I can speak, he touches my forehead with his finger, and everything goes black.

Chapter 8

The Orgy Room

Dreams race through my head—memories, nightmares, my parents, still alive, all standing in a sunny field. There are flowers. We were never in a field full of flowers, so it must be a dream. There's the lake, and the beach! My friends are there, my companions, my lover's. I know it's just a dream but it seems so real. I embrace it. Anything for a chance to see them again. Anything for a chance to feel their touch on my skin. I can feel their warmth against my body. The pleasure helps me. My mind is spinning as each movement plays out before me. The memories stream by, like clouds blown by a strong wind. I reach for them, but they slip through my fingers, melting away into nothingness. Again, I feel the pain, over and over. I want to cover my eyes, but I can't. The feelings are pouring out of me. My whole world feels like it's crashing down around me. Darkness creeps in from the edges as I watch them fade to dust, and then it's black again.

I am vaguely aware that I am moving. Or, to be correct, I am on something that is moving. As I piece together my surroundings, I can tell my head is covered, small pinpricks of light here and there. It's a heavy fabric covering my head. The musty smell of spittle and sweat fills my nostrils. These bastards couldn't even use a clean sack. Thoughts of the poor souls who were unfortunate to don this hood before me are quickly abated as whatever vehicle I am lying in the back of hits a large hole in the trail and I am jolted to my senses. I struggle to move, but my hands and legs are tied. I hear a moan over the metallic rattle of my transport and realize I am actually tied to another person. I crane my neck to try and catch a glimpse through the tattered fabric of who my traveling companion might be but to no avail. The vehicle slows to a stop. I can hear voices approaching.

"See, I told you I saw her moving," one voice mutters in a low gruff tone.

"Well, that's not supposed to happen," the second dryer voice replies.

As I try to strain to see my captors, I see a shadow move in front of me, then a sharp blow, and darkness again. No dreams this time, just a splitting headache.

I have no idea how much time passes before I awake.

"Mother fuckers…" I mutter to myself, rubbing my hand over the large bump I now have on my forehead. It occurs to me my hands are not bound. In fact, I don't seem to be restrained at all.

As light floods the thin slits, my eyes dare open. I begin to piece together my situation. It's a weird green light, warm but menacing. It almost feels like it is bathing my entire body in its glow. I rub my eyes and instantly realize I am surrounded by my previous captors. I also realize I am naked. I sit up too fast and through a dizzy haze I can feel the pounding lump on my head. I reach out and touch it, gingerly. Unable to stop myself I yell out angrily "Which ever of you cock sucking inbred little dick having mother fuckers hit me on the head, I'm going to cut your tiny little rat balls off and shove them down your god damn throat!"

There is muffled laughter somewhere off to my right and as my vision clears and my eyes adjust to the light, soon I'm able to take in my surroundings.

For a second, I think I am in another dream. The room is almost identical to the mountain bunker, only bathed in a pale green glow instead of the warm soft white light. There are dozens of people, naked like me. all on soft beds of pillows. Some still lying down, others trying to stand—a few with the same dazed look I imagine adorns my face. There are dozens of little boner men, identical to my friend in the mountain, running around to each person—bringing them food and drink, washing them, tending to the bumps and bruises we all seem to share. There's even a few giving foot massages.

Now I am just completely confused.

I feel a cold sensation on the bump on my forehead and instantly move to slap it away. The little man falls to his knees, begging me for my forgiveness.

"You should be nice to the trolls. They only want to help."

A tall dark figure stands before me. His torso is outlined by the glowing light behind him. He cuts quite a figure, at six foot two or three, strong build with massive shoulders and thick arms. Not unlike my deceased lover, his presence brings an aura of respect and fear.

"You'll excuse my manners, but I'm a bit picky about who I let touch me when I'm sitting naked in a strange room full of weird people, some of whom I assume are responsible for abducting me and giving me this beauty mark," I snark as I point to the bulge on my head, with as much sass as I can muster.

My retort summons a hearty chuckle from the man.

"They said you were a handful. I'm glad to see that they were not exaggerating. Please, let the little man tend to you then I will show you what you have gotten yourself into. And don't worry about the two that brought you here. They are currently resting on top of a large pile of ants outside, sans skin. I think you'll agree their punishment fits their crime."

And with that he turns and walks away. As the light hits his face I gasp. It could have been his twin, but the likeness was more than that. He was a carbon copy of my lover. I moved to get up and go after him, but several little hands hold me back, and soon he disappears from view.

The little hands pamper my body. As my muscles are rubbed and my skin cleaned, my mind is racing. What the actual fuck is going on? Who was that and what are these people getting prepped for? This is not the cave I remembered as a little girl. And this sure as fuck seems like a lot of effort to go through just to make a bunch of future batteries happy. The cool cloth returns to my head, soothing the lump. As the pain subsides, I feel myself relaxing. My mind fights it at first, but it's no use. The hands are magic all over my body. Every touch releases me from the tension, separates me from the bonds of stress and anger. No matter how hard I try I can't focus on anything but the tiny fingers working every inch of my skin—dozens of points on my body all coaxing pleasure out of my weary hide. I lean back into my pillows, letting the little men take me away. My mind is awash with the pleasure of their hands carrying me. I feel like I'm floating on a cloud of ecstasy. By the time we reach the pool in the center of the room I am completely overcome by the sensations. I feel lust building in me, aching to be set free. My mind is blank aside from these strange unexplainable desires flooding over me. From across the pool I see a man, about my height and thinly built, his scrawny frame shaved bare, aside from the curly blonde hair on his head. His body is diminutive, almost fragile, you could say. Still, I am drawn to his erection, huge and pulsing, easily twice the length of my hand and too large for me to wrap my fingers all the way around. I'm entranced by it; I move towards him at the center of the pool. Impulsively, I go for his manhood. I want it. The feeling of his hard cock filling both my hands is tremendous. I glow with unexpected excitement as I caress his engorged member. He stands like a statue, quietly moaning with pleasure as I pull and twist at his rod. I am so distracted I don't notice another man has slipped in beside me, almost identical to the first, only dark straight hair. As his equally impressive cock enters my view, I reach for it, wanting to feel the power of holding both men in my grasp. I gently take the second man's rod in my palm, and as I close my fingers around his shaft they are met by the fingers of the blonde. I catch his gaze as he stares longingly at the meat between his fingers and feel myself getting even more aroused. My gentle stroking is interrupted by large hands on my back, gently sliding around to my breasts then the feeling of them pulling their body tight to mine. Another well-endowed suitor, I discover. He has a similar physique, by the feel of it. Apparently, our host has a type. I lean into this new interloper, enjoying the rush of his hands exploring my body. As I release my previous interest from my grip, the blonde drops to his knees and begins stroking his new companion with both hands. Watching his hands work the shaft, I am dripping. I desire to be penetrated, but I want to see more. The dark-haired man moans with the pleasure he is receiving at every stroke.

I can hear myself mumbling, "Suck it. I want to see you suck it so bad!"

Without hesitation, the blonde leans forward and lets the cock slide past his lips, only taking an inch or two at first, letting his jaw adjust to the enormous endeavor he is about to undertake. I move in close to watch the member disappear behind those thin pink lips. The sounds of subtle gagging fills my ears and pleases my mind. The hands pull me against the chest of the man behind me. I lean into him completely now, giving into the unexplainable and uncontrollable desire—wanting, needing him to fill me.

"I want your fingers to please me," I whisper, as if another person is controlling my body and my mind is only a spectator.

He is happy to oblige. His massive cock pressed into my back, I reach behind me and grab it just as his fingertip brushes the outside of my labia. I shudder and try to push forward but he teases me, tracing every fold and pressing into my mound gently before pulling his hand tight against me. The pressure blossoms the petal of my flower and his skillful touch draws out the moisture in me, covering his fingers as he spreads my lips and runs a long digit past my hungry pussy. Pressing hard enough to make me squirm then releasing me and driving downwards into my wetness. I'm distracted from his teasing fingers by his soft lips on my neck. He teases my hard nipples and squeezes my breasts, adding to the burning lust inside me. The two men in front of me are lost in their own passion. The hungry blonde trying his best to choke down every inch of his partner's considerable package. The latter lacing his fingers through the blonde's curls, grabbing a handful and pulling his head down further, forcing his throat to completely engulf his masculinity. I am gushing, feeling yet another set of hands on my body as a fourth twink joins us, similar in body but less gifted between his legs. He takes his position in front of me, and before I can move him from blocking my view he is on his knees. His hands pull apart my legs, his fingers pressing into my skin as they run down my thighs. I feel his hot breath arousing me, teasing, tempting me. I want his tongue and I grab his head to force him in. The hand is gone, and I moan as his tongue presses wide and firm against my pussy. Long firm strokes of the tip followed by sucking in my clit and letting it run between his teeth back to me. He shakes his head vigorously thrashing his tongue back and forth, dipping inside me to tease out more of my sweetness then making impossible circles around every edge and expertly flicking the tip across every layer, driving me wild.

The show in front of me is reaching its climax. The blonde is looking up, longing for the dark-haired man's seed in his mouth. Loud moaning and violent hip thrusts are followed by heavy exaggerated breathing as the dark-haired man explodes in the mouth of his eager companion. The thick hot cum drips from around his shaft and the lips of the receiver and down his chin, into the water. The Blonde fully extracts the cock from his mouth, shifting his stance and positioning the other man behind him, kissing the cum to him, bathing their tongues in it. For a moment I am jealous, wiping some of the cum from the blonde's chin with my finger then sucking it clean. The men both smile with approval. The hunger is still filling their eyes. The two men take turns kissing me as I try to maintain balance with the third and fourth. They gently lower me onto a pillow beside the pool. The man resumes eating my pussy with a voracious desperation and a wild willingness of his tongue. The other two men return to their spent partner, still breathing heavily, his cock now growing tired and limp. The two flank the man, running their hands over his body, teasing him. Finally, the man in front grabs his hair, pulling his open mouth towards his waiting cock. The dark-haired man's knees are stiff, he bends at the waist allowing the blonde to slip in behind him. His muffled moans barely escape around the cock filling the dark-haired man's mouth as the blonde easily presses his manhood into the dark hole of the man he so recently let complete in his mouth. Slow at first, the rhythmic pumping increases in velocity and speed, forcing himself further into the dark-haired man. The dark-haired man gives completely into the rhythm but then the blonde's thrusts push him forward, his mouth deeper on to the final man's cock. The three men moan excitedly with each movement and thrust, pounding their companion back and forth between them. The man in the middle grows hard again, the pleasure of being used by the two men waking inside of him a more primal urge to please and be pleased. The inexplicable pleasure of watching the three men ravish each other only adds to the satisfaction of the talented tongue between my legs, bringing me close, fingers now also working to fulfill me. I can't orgasm. Not yet. I want to watch these two men fill the third with their cum and feel the delight of their semen exploding out of his orifices.

Both men let out a primordial moan as they cum, thrusting deep into the man and holding their gushing members inside him as shot after shot of their thick jizz fills him, soon running down his face and legs. The man whimpers in hungry disappointment, obviously wanting more as the cocks slip out of him, and the two other men collapse onto the pillows besides the pool, quickly cleaned and scrubbed by a set of little boner men. The middle man stands now, clearly enjoying the salty treat filling his mouth and delighted at his success as the cum runs down his face, chest and legs. Another group of little men come to clean him but are waved into retreat by a young couple who hungrily lap at the juice on his legs and ass, working their way up till their faces meet his erect manhood. The gentleman of the couple continues to follow the trail to its source, driving his tongue deep into the man's ass, while she vigorously takes his cock into both hands and strokes it feverishly, teasing the tip with her tongue. Moaning with pleasure, the man's knees shake as the couple delights in raising him to full attention and enthusiastically attempt to drain him of his remaining fluids. I am so caught up watching the show that I don't feel the well-endowed stranger move in behind me until he lifts me onto his lap. His massive cock slips surprisingly easily into my dripping snatch. I catch myself letting out a loud "oo oh" as his cock stretches me wide open.

My pussy attendant yelps with glee as he watches the massive tool disappear inside me. Before it can be withdrawn for a second thrust, he buries his face back into my pussy, delighting at the feel of both my pussy lips and the man's tool sliding on his tongue. I close my eyes, letting the sensation of the two men working over my cunt wash across my body. I can feel my clit pulsing, begging for more, the walls of my vagina stretched and filled. Each rhythmic thrust brings me further towards total ecstasy. I can feel the furious movement of his tongue as it passes seamlessly from my clit to the anxious cock penetrating me. The moans from the as yet unseen body thrusting his cock in and out of me are deep and sensual. His grip on my body tightens as his pleasure overwhelms him. Two strong hands grip me tight, bouncing me harder and harder down on his enormous appendage. My pussy attendant can't keep up and breathlessly retreats, replacing his tongue with two fingers. Rubbing and pressing my clit in a frantic but purposeful fashion, responding to every movement I make, every sound I emit, like I am directing him with my hips.

I hear loud, soulful screams of a woman at the verge of orgasm. I open my eyes to see the three in front of me have changed position. She is between the two men now. Both are standing. I look closer and can see they are both inside her, each penetrating a different hole. They thrust upward in unison, lifting her tiny body off the ground completely. As she floats between them, she rocks her hips, working their cocks deeper and deeper into her as she digs her fingernails into the man she is facing. Her cries of pleasure tinged with a hint of pain echo across the room. She tries biting her lip to quiet herself, but a deep push has her throwing her head back crying out even louder!

I am hypnotized by the display in front of me, as is the faceless cock inside me. His vigorous pounding has turned to a slow rocking of just his hips—slipping himself slowly in and out of me—pulling his tip completely out and then presses back into me.

Several women approach us. Tall, perfectly proportioned goddesses. walking in a determined manner straight toward us. Three of the women break off and head for the tripod in front of us. The other trio joins us.

I watch as two of the women don strap-ons and move into position behind the men, carefully lubing their toys and then entering the men mercilessly. Their powerful and unexpected penetrating jabs push the men to their tippy toes and lift the impaled body of the young lady even higher. The third looks bemused and forcefully grabs the girl's hair, pulling it back hard, stifling her surprised and excited cries by jamming her tongue down her throat. She twists the girl's nipples hard, letting her cry out as her mouth is now moving to the girl's breast. We make eye contact as the woman bites the girl's nipple, causing another verbal outburst. She holds my gaze as her hand slides to the girl's crotch, first letting two of her fingers split across the pulsating cock pressed into her then slipping them in alongside it. Stretching her wider. The girl bites her lip again, almost unable to make a sound as she is brought to her limit. Still holding my stare, the woman smiles—a devilish grin. She adjusts the angle of her wrists so her thumb can now easily rub the clit of this writhing pincushion she now holds in her control. She signals the two women on either side and they begin vigorously pounding away the now mostly motionless men. Completely lost in ecstasy, both men are thoroughly submissive to these new master's working them like puppets, forcing their will onto and into them. The men's bodies wind and moan from the pain of the artificial tools slamming hard inside them, often biting the girl to keep from being overcome by the sensations rising through their bodies, turning from pain to pleasure. Both men's moans grow louder as their master's force them to the brink of cumming. The third woman holds my stare as she yanks back the girl's hair again, her eyes teasing me the way her thumb is teasing the clit of the puppet at the end of her fingers. I can tell she is bringing her right to the brink of an orgasm then holding her there. With a devilish curiosity, I watch as she keeps the poor girl at the brink, legs shaking, breathing hard and fast and in short bursts, begging her puppeteer to let her come. It isn't until the two men simultaneously explode in her swollen orifices the puppeteer allows her to climax with a few vigorous, talented movements of her wrist. She has the girl shaking and screaming as the orgasm takes control of her body. The woman doesn't stop. She keeps the girl rocking out of control until her pussy squirts into her hand. She pulls her hand away, licking some of the cum off her fingers. Her eyes show how pleased she is with herself as she turns and walks away. Her two accomplices release their three puppets and they all collapse in a cum soaked heap to the side. Almost instantly, the little boner men are there to clean and tend to them.

Watching the three of them climax while being so brutally violated and used has me beyond invigorated. I realize my hips have been rocking violently on the lap of the faceless cock inside me. Watching her control them like puppets has me close to cumming, and I work to restrain myself. The owner of the tool inside me does not. I suddenly feel his strong hands grip my hips, pulling me down hard as his body convulses upwards. The shock of this sudden deep penetration excites me further but before I can reach climax, I feel him burst inside me. I can feel each load of hot jizz painting my insides until it drips, warm and thick, out of me along his pulsating shaft. He releases my hips and shrinks away.

The three women surrounding me have been waiting patiently for him to finish so they could have their turn with me. The unseen man carefully removes himself from me, lifting me off him with ease and setting me down on the pillows next to us. He slips away unseen and I bask in the thought of never knowing his face—just a strong body and massive cock. I start to muse internally about how much better sex with men would be if all encounters could be faceless, when I feel a familiar tongue licking my twat clean. It's my pussy attendant from earlier, come to finish the job he started. Only this time he has help. While two of the ladies settle in comfortably next to me, allowing their hands to gently begin exploring my body, the third has the twink by the hair, aggressively directing him where to lick, making sure he sucks up every last drop. At first, I don't realize where her other hand is, but when the twink misses a spot I watch her flex her forearm and I suddenly realize her fist is up his ass all the way to the wrist!

The twink finishes his job and then excitedly begs for more. The two ladies to my side quickly lift my legs straight up and back, leaving my ass hole exposed. The third woman releases the twink's hair and thrusts him forward with her arm. The twink dives into my ass, eagerly licking around it, flicking with just the tip of his tongue, then pressing firmly in. The sensation is mind blowing, and I don't even try to resist. I want more and hear myself begging for it. My hungry pleas do not go unnoticed and the twink slips a single digit in alongside his tongue—carefully at first—just one knuckle, then two.

 I am moaning incoherently now, this forbidden sensation releasing the last of my resistance and inhibitions. I am putty in their hands and want them to do whatever they desire with me. The two women to my side seize the opportunity. Releasing my legs, I let my feet drop and rest gently on the twink's back. Soft hands caress my body. I can feel each fingertip magically glide across my skin, leaving an excited trail of goosebumps in their wake. Gentle lips are next, on my neck, my shoulder, on my own lips. As one mouth moves to my breast, I feel another press her lips to mine, her tongue gently parting them to gain entry to my mouth. My own tongue greets hers anxiously, and I find myself gripping the back of her head, holding her to me tightly, not wanting to let her slip away. She's not going anywhere, and she cradles my head to hers as well, allowing our passionate embrace to continue indefinitely.

I feel the twink's body tense and shake as the third woman buries her fist deep inside him. With a tiny whimper, he drops weakly into the pool, cumming as he falls. She removes her fist from the twink, nonchalantly, as if she was just pulling her hand out of her pocket. Several little men surround the two of them, cleaning her and removing the still cooing twink from the pool and laying him carefully out onto the pillows before attending to him. The satisfied smile on his face as he drifts off to sleep is inspiration enough for me to just go with it. Not that I could resist now, even if I wanted too. My body is so overcome, it's a sensory overload. I feel like a puppet in these ladies' hands and I am hungrily soaking up every pleasurable second!

My attention is briefly drawn to several of the other moaning piles of bodies in the room. Some just a passionate display of one on one, girl on guy, guy on guy, girl on girl—all of the combinations that two people can make. Mostly, it's hard to tell who is involved. So many arms and legs intertwined, cocks sliding into any orifice, pussies full of fingers and tongues, so many holes being penetrated by two or more cocks at once. It doesn't seem to matter what your gender or preference. Here, there is plenty of everything to satisfy every want and need. Handcuffs, dildoes, whips, ties. It's all happening all around, and everyone is becoming lost in the overwhelming pleasure of it all. As each person cums and collapses, they are immediately tended to by the little men. Cleaned, comforted and put to rest. It's a stark contrast to my last visit to these tunnels.

My attention doesn't wander for long. The three ladies are intent on bringing me to orgasm and I quickly find my focus as the first finger presses against my outer petals. I quiver with anticipation as a gentle hand teases the outside of my lips. I want to grab her hand and force her fingers into me, but I can't. Two of the women are holding my arms, keeping me outstretched, totally at their mercy. My body begs to be penetrated. The soft lips of my two constrainers explore all the parts of my body they can reach from their positions at my side. Everything below the waist, however, seems to be the territory of the woman who destroyed the twink. I close my eyes, fantasizing about how she wrecked him and made him cum so hard he passed out. I want that. I want to be fucked so hard I can't breathe, so satisfied I collapse into a useless pile for the little men to clean up.

 Both her hands are teasing me now. Strong fingers run up and down my inner thigh, finally stopping at my dripping wet flower, carefully pulling my petals apart. I want to watch her press her face into me but the other two have me pinned, pulling my hair back, taking turns forcing their tongues into my mouth, barely allowing my muffled moans to escape much less my pleas to have her inside me. I am bursting, finally feeling her hot breath on my clit, her soft skin and long hair brushing my legs as she moves in. The two pull my legs apart, allowing the third unfettered access to my center. Her fingers still have me spread wide open and as her tongue brushes my clit for the first time, I cry out. The pleasure is overwhelming. So much anticipation has me on edge and now this perfect tongue is gently satisfying me. So slow and soft at first, but that quickly turns to vigorous well-timed strokes on my noble button, driving me wild. She lets two fingers slip inside me while sucking my clit into her mouth. I convulse uncontrollably, wanting more and wanting it harder! She obliges me, slipping a third finger in while pinching my clit between two digits with her other hand, forcing my button out allowing her tongue unlimited access. I am completely at her mercy and continue to thrash uncontrollably as my body is overcome by the all-consuming ecstasy. The two women at my side move to cover more of my body with their soft lips. My hands and forearms are free, and I desperately grab at their soft but firm bodies, letting my hands run down their backs then up their legs. My fingers quickly find their target. Both women gasp and moan as I enter them, their cunts sopping wet, betraying their desire. Two fingers slip into each easily, my thumbs quickly finding their clits. I work my digits in rhythm to the puppet master controlling my own movements, her skilled mouth lavishing pleasure on me. Our buddies move in unison, one undulating mass moving toward orgasm. I try to keep the pace but can't focus with the overwhelming sensation's rocking my body from its very core. The girl to my right breaks first, biting hard into my shoulder, her nails digging into my skin. Her vagina clenches my finger, and I put all my energy into vigorously pushing her over the top. It only takes a second before I feel her hips rock as she creams into my hand. She comes hard, popping her hips up and down for several seconds before her knees get weak and she starts to fall, exhausted and satisfied to the pillows.

She quickly regains her composure, however ,and grabs a dildo from the table I hadn't even noticed was there before. As she positions herself between my legs with her companion, the other woman moves over the top of me, her legs once again pinning my arms, leaving her neat little box just over my face. She grabs me by the hair and pulls my face into her. I don't even try to resist, and my tongue is out before my face reaches her inner garden. The sweet juice from her pussy is like nectar on my tongue. I hungrily lick her, inside and out. She holds my head to her with both hands as she grinds on my face. I can barely breathe but don't care, the feeling of my tongue dancing across her excited clit then sliding into her and out, painting her lips with their own sweet essence, is exhilarating!

I want more and force my face harder against her mound. Her body rocks as I send wave after wave of spine-tingling pleasure through her. She is riding my face, overcome by her own ecstasy, unable to contribute to the others working my pussy into a fervor. The puppeteer's fingers penetrate me and pull me wide open. Her thumbs lift my hood leaving my clit bare, exposed to the voracious tongue of the third woman as she works her oral muscle around the toy she unceasingly thrust in and out of my eager pussy. Her long hair falling softly on my abdomen, gently exciting me and adding to the already overwhelming sensations crashing through my body. It's more than I can handle. I throw my head back, releasing her pussy lips from my teeth's grip, moaning and writhing uncontrollably. The two ladies seize the opportunity and work the dildo harder and faster, each stroke sending a tsunami of crazy tingling warmth through me. I feel myself changing from loving it to needing it. Oh, God. More. I want more! I can't help it. I Cry out.

"Please, don't stop. Please, please, don't stop!" I beg.

My words invigorate them. Their energy seems endless, their skills at exploring my pussy seem limitless. I am in ecstasy, writhing, dripping, begging for more. I can feel fingers start to probe my third hole. It's almost too much. I know if she presses her finger into me I will cum. Part of me wants her to wait—to let this crazy pleasure train continue forever. A bigger part wants to cum. I am at my limit and the need to orgasm is all consuming.

"Yes, put it in. Fuck my ass, make me cum. I want to cum so bad!"

The words don't even sound like my own. Feeble and weak, I never beg for anything, but for this I'm willing to do just about everything. My surprise at my own vulnerability is quickly put out of my mind as a finger slips into my ass.

"Oh fuck" I yell loudly as my body shakes and convulses. The orgasm spreads quickly through me. From my very center to the tips of my fingers and toes, every muscle in my body twitches and relaxes simultaneously as wave after wave of euphoria crashes across my torso, up my neck, and across my face. It's so all-encompassing, even my hair tingles. The ladies slowly withdraw from me, each movement sending more pleasing tingles through my body. They do not leave, however, carefully kissing and caressing me, letting my body slowly settle as the tide of ecstasy ebbs away, leaving me feeling spent and satisfied.

As I ease into the pillows, my two nearly spent entertainers quickly find themselves in a sixty-nine position. Pleasing me has them both extremely aroused and it doesn't take long before their loud moans fill the air. I watch contently as they satiate their own lust by the selfless act of one satisfying the other. I find myself getting aroused again as I watch the two bodies entwine in such a sensual series of motions. I can't help but to gently touch myself, giving me pleasing chills. The two know each other's bodies well, and they soon convulse their bodies against each other, their faces locked into each other's most delicate areas and their tongues never ceasing. It's an extremely impressive and erotic site to behold. As they reach their climax both women seem to cum together. A beautiful sight that I relish as I let my fingers find myself, and I am surprised to feel that I am wet anew. I grab the dildo nearest me and put it to work, closing my eyes. Thoughts of all the amazingly erotic things I have seen play like a movie through my mind. Unable to control it, images of the madam begin to filter in, memories of the beach, of all the interludes in the bunker, even of just holding her close to me. At first, I am taken aback, but the memories are too clear, too tangible to just be fantasies. I want them to be real so bad I don't fight it or even try to understand it. As I drift further away, further into the memories, my hands work the dildo, tickling my clit—teasing my insides. I can almost feel her touch. Oh, how I miss the way she would make my body explode, one orgasm after another!

I feel it building, the same way it would build when she touched me. I feel the same rush of excitement and anticipation that I would get whenever her mouth was on my skin. I manipulate the toy faster, letting the penetrating vibrating parts take me away to her. My mind is lost as I fantasize of her pressing her beautiful naked body against mine, her pussy to my lips as her lips in turn please me. I can almost taste her on my tongue, almost smell her sweet scent. Further down into the fantasy I slip, desperately wishing she was here—wishing she could have had all these hands on her like I did, all these people watching, aching to feel her wet juices, lusting to feel her gentle lips against their skin as I did, living to please her as she so deserved. The more intense the fantasy becomes, the more real the feel of her touch seems to be. I am bursting, completely lost in a false world that has brought us back together. She is with me and we are just creatures to be pleased by the masses. It's so clear, we are face to face. She on her back, me over her as two faceless bodies insert their cocks, filling us both perfectly. My pleasure is directly linked to hers as these faceless bodies pound us in unison. I can see it in her face. The look I have strived so hard to give her so many times when we were together. We are nearing orgasm.

She pulls me down to her and whispers to me. "I want your tongue!"

The faceless figures drop to their knees. Impossibly soft feminine tongues explore us. The feeling is incredible. Completely lost in the fantasy, I allow myself to be there, believing I am there with her in this moment. I call out her name as the mysterious tongues do wonderful things to us.

She reaches up and pulls my lips to hers, kissing me long and passionately. I can feel the energy passing between us. I am consumed by the overwhelming excitement just like I did with our first kiss. She continues to hold me. Our tongues are going wild now. I kiss her, desperate to remember every last detail of her lips, how they feel against mine. It's too much, I can't control it. As she pulls my hair, forcing me closer to her, we both cum. An explosive mind blowing, toe curling, out of this world, over the top, orgasm. Just like the night at the lake. I feel the same incredible energy rush through my body followed by indescribable pleasure, wiping me out completely. I know she will disappear the second I lose my focus, the second I crash back to reality. To my surprise, she pulls my head close to hers, and for a moment everything freezes. I am only aware of our two energies passing effortlessly between each other. She places her hands on the sides of my face, locking her eyes on mine.

I am frozen as she smiles and calmly whispers, "You have my energy. I will always be with you. We are right here watching over you. Just close your eyes. I will be here, waiting for you. I am forever yours and with you!"

I can feel her starting to fade as the orgasm ebbs. My eyes well with tears, not from sadness but from joy. I can feel that was so much more than a fantasy. For a moment we were together and I know that as long as I live, I will carry her with me. I know we will be together again. I let myself relax and watch as she disappears. The fog in my mind is quickly wearing thin, and I know when I open my eyes I will be in a different place, both mentally and physically. I'm excited now, knowing I can share my body with her just by closing my eyes, and I can share my new friends with her for however long I am locked in this weird world, seemingly designed solely for providing pleasure. I don't know the reasons for it, but for the moment I really don't care!

One last deep breath and I open my eyes, half expecting to be in an empty room or surrounded by the governor's evil henchmen, but I am not. I'm still in the fuck room. As I settle onto the pillows, completely spent, I am aware of the little men approaching.

"Back to work boys."

Quite pleased with myself, I carefully close my eyes again, this time just to enjoy the feeling of being completely satisfied. I think to myself, *"I could get used to this life."*

I have no idea how short lived it will be.

Chapter 9

Victory?

My muscles ache as my body settles. Even with my eyes closed I can see the rhythmic pulsating bodies entangled all around me. The familiar tingle of excitement still burns inside me as I lay naked in the center of the room. In my mind, I feel as though all eyes are on me and I relish in the pleasure of being the center of attention. Even though I feel completely spent my mind is still lusting for more—more hands caressing my skin, more mouths kissing every inch of me, more tongues pleasing me, more cocks penetrating me. I lay still. just fantasizing about being completely enveloped by the mass of bodies all around me. My pussy is getting wetter and wetter the more I dream. The oddly familiar feeling of small hands softly but thoroughly scrubbing and cleaning my skin brings me out of my haze with a snap. The odd little men, identical to the little boner man I befriended in the cave in what seems like an eternity ago, are gently wiping me clean and massaging my sore muscles back to life. I'm too exhausted to question it any longer. In my mind I know I am here for a reason, but that reason is just a faded memory now. The pleasure has consumed me. I just lay my head back and enjoy the experience. A relaxing calm settles over my body. I feel myself almost drift off to sleep when I hear a familiar voice.

"Someone looks happy."

It's the clone of my lover. My mind is racing, and suddenly everything comes rushing back to me. Him, the madam, even my mission. I still don't know what to make of this man. Part of me wants to embrace him, give him the trust that his counterpart had worked so hard to earn. Another part wants to destroy him—make him suffer for dishonoring the memory of someone so close to me, someone who was willing to sacrifice their very being just so I would have a chance to live. Twice!

He doesn't give me the chance to decide.

"Come with me," he commands abruptly.

"Where?" I asked simply.

"There is someone you need to meet," he replies, almost annoyed I would ask.

I stand and the little men dress me in my skirt and corset, notably missing all the weapons. Smart, I suppose, but still odd they would take the time to bother at all considering the situation I'm in.

I follow the clone to the back of the room. Behind several bolts of cloth stands a well-hidden door that, seemingly like magic, opens as we approach. The dim lights that flicker on as we enter the hall reveal a horror show of bodies hanging from the wall. I keep pace, not wanting him to see my fear at the grotesque display all around us. He must sense it. Without turning, he points to a corpse in the wall.

"Recognize this douche bag?" he quips

As my eyes adjust to the light and I can see more clearly, I realize it's the pointy tooth bastard that brought me here. Several, in fact. Unable to resist any longer I risk a glance around the hall. It's like a body storage for every evil, murderous psycho I have ever encountered, and there are dozens of them. Just hanging there like empty sacks of meat waiting to be filled with anger and hate.

Almost without realizing it I mutter, "What the actual fuck"?

He doesn't respond. Instead, he keeps leading me forward. As we near the end of the hall, another door becomes visible. This one is clearly leading to a brightly lit room as evidenced by the glow emitting from around the edges. The door swings open and the clone steps aside, motioning for me to go in. I pause, thinking he is going to lead me inside. He smiles bleakly.

"No meat puppets past this point," he stammers, almost disappointed in himself at his own self-awareness. I continue to hesitate. "If he wanted something bad to happen to you it would have happened already," he says impatiently, now clearly annoyed that I'm acting so skeptical.

Accepting I have no other option, I step through the door and into the light. As I walk forward, the door closes behind me and seems to disappear into the wall. The entire room is a shapeless glowing ball of light. I can't tell if it's big or small, tall or short. I can't even tell where the floor ends and the walls begin. I continue forward, each step even more timid than the last. The disorienting nature of the room is getting to me. I can't even tell which way is up anymore, so I stop, feeling helpless and lost. I want to call out, but I know it is pointless. So, I stand with my eyes closed trying to orientate myself.

"Not much to see with your eyes closed."

The voice echoes across the room. I open my eyes to try to discern its source. I'm still alone, but the room is changing. The light dims and I am standing on the beach by the lake. I feel the sand between my toes, the cool breeze from the water, even the smell of the plants and trees. As I turn, it's like I'm completely immersed back to that wonderful place.

I can feel the tears forming in the corners of my eyes. Powerful emotions flood my body. This place, so much happened here, so much joy, and so much loss. Why this place? How did he know, and more importantly how is this possible? The governor is just supposed to be a nobody who got lucky. No one mentioned he could do any of this. My pain quickly turns to anger as the idea that he would use this place as some elaborate trick to get me to let my guard down. I clench my fists and squeeze my eyes shut.

"You fucking asshole, you have no right!" I yell at the top of my lungs.

I feel the cool breeze change to the hot sandy wind of the desert against my skin. When I open my eyes, there is just Wasteland surrounding me. A figure approaches me from the dust, a withered man in a suit. I can see him clearly, almost as if the sand doesn't touch him. Instead, it swirls carefully around him. The air and light seem to bend around him. I can see him clear as day, but I can't make out a single distinguishing feature. It's like he is just appearing, like a figure out of a dream that never seems quite real—someone who seems familiar while you're asleep, but you can't remember anything about them when you wake up.

"I am sorry about the lake. Human emotions tend to elude me. I know it is a place that brought you happiness. I did not mean to cause you pain." He speaks in an odd monotone, completely devoid of any inflection.

"What the fuck is this, and why am I here?!" I ask.

"You are here to lead the revolution." He replies, dryly.

I can feel the dumbfounded look fall across my face despite my best efforts to remain stern.

He continues. "You have been told part of the story but almost none of the truth—starting with me, and more importantly who you really are and why you are so special."

"You're responsible for the death of everyone I have ever cared about, and now you want me to sit here and listen to your sob story just because you have a magic room?" I quiz him.

A troubled look comes over his face.

"The room is not magic," he states, matter of factly.

I'm dumbfounded. "Everything I just accused you of, and you got stuck on my description of your decorating choices!" I yell. I feel the anger building, my body tensing. I don't know how but I really want to kick this ambiguous looking mother fucker's ass.

"You cannot *kick my ass*. I am not real, nor is any of this."

I'm taken aback by his ability to seemingly know what I'm thinking. Before I can respond, he raises his hand and snaps his fingers. The world disappears and I find myself standing in a room full of machines and blinking lights with an even more shadowy version of the man in front of me.

"It is all just a hologram. Me, the landscape, the wind, the smells, even the taste of the sand in your mouth—all of it just a light I can use to trick your mind into seeing what I want it to."

I stammer, "Where...I mean how-"

He cuts me off. "I, if you want to call me that, am just a hologram projected by the machine behind me. I am actually a combination of millions of psyches collected, stored, and absorbed into one in that giant green glowing jar. What you were told about 'I' being a lucky janitor is just the first of many lies you and everyone else were told to keep order and peace in the five regions. What you said about 'I' killing everyone you've ever cared about also is not true."

Rage flows through my body. I can feel the dark energy burning inside of me. *I just need an opening and this mother fucker is going down.*"

"Your lover and the madam were destroyed by The Five for giving you too much power. Terminated in their last moments by the very machine that created this world. Turned to dust so you would not be able to save them or revive them later. To be fair, however, I would have destroyed them myself if that was what was necessary to get you here. As for your parents I did have them killed, only under direct orders from the five. Your parents are the reason you were chosen."

He seems to notice my body tensing, preparing to strike. An unimpressed look spreads across is face. The closest thing to an emotion I can expect. He continues with his speech.

"As it turns out, however, absorbing their consciousness is how you ended up escaping in the beginning and the reason 'I' have decided to choose you to lead the rebellion. That, and to be perfectly honest, you destroyed all of the other potential candidates when you and your lover ruined my dolls. So, please. Listen to what I have to say and then decide if you still want to poison me with that dark energy you are holding. It will not kill me. Instead, it will cause me to lose my own self-awareness and fall back under The Five's control, as just a machine designed for punishing their enemies."

I am taken aback again by his ability to get into my head, to see what I am planning.

"I will begin with what you were told about the two different energies. That part is basically true. And, thanks to several of the wiser consciousness' I have absorbed, I have been able to create a way to consume positive or light energy without destroying the host. Hence, the orgy you involuntarily enjoyed so much when you got here."

"You killed my parents and felt bad, so you got me laid so I would start a war?" I ask in disbelief.

"No, when I killed your parents their positive energy was the tipping point to my becoming fully self-aware. As I was grappling with my new reality, your mother's consciousness was able to override the default setting in one of the drone bodies. When I tried to destroy her and the drone, I was unable to control the flow of energy, thanks to your father and the drone controlled by your mom rescued you from becoming absorbed. Once outside with no obstructions between it and the satellites, the drone was susceptible to reprogramming by The Five and they, having realized my own functions were compromised, deleted your mother's consciousness from the drone, reprogramming him and setting in motion events that brought you here now."

"I'm listening," I say. Every muscle in my body wants to attack. My heart is black with hatred. My body is poised to strike. There's just so many questions in my mind, I need to know more than I need vengeance. This machine knows what happened and I'm going to get the answers— whether it tells me now or I suck them out of its last dying circuit.

"The drone you refer to as your lover is a seek and destroy model. I used it for missions sent down to me from The Five. As you have seen, I have several. But the one your mother manipulated left here without it's firewall in place—a sort of safety lock for his programming that keeps outside sources from affecting it. Instead, it was allowed to develop a consciousness of its own based on the information The Five fed to it, along with the few memories your mother's consciousness left in him. Rare, but not unheard of. In fact, after your escape I allowed a similar model here to develop its own self-awareness so I could better understand it's movements. Needless to say, with a clone out wreaking havoc among the people I had to retire the rest of that model of drone. It would be chaos to have an enemy unit identical to any of my own.

Just the security precautions necessary would be outrageous."

"This all would have been a lot easier if he could have just walked back in here and torn the place to shreds."

"That information, along with feelings it developed for you, created the charming personality you came to know so well. His desire to be rid of the haunting memories are what drove him to try and seek out and destroy me. His methods were a gift from The Five to try to regain control of me."

"You said you had my mother and father's consciousness. They were killed out in the desert, not here in your cave. They couldn't have been absorbed by you." My accusatory tone not registering the slightest effect on the face of the machine.

"The drone with the pointy teeth is a model I designed specifically to temporarily absorb and store the energies and bring them back to me. He basically lobotomized your parents before he allowed them to be murdered."

"And all those girls we rescued, all those people we killed, was just some dark vendetta my lover had to annoy you? Is that what you're trying to tell me?"

"No. The vessels you released were natural born sources of positive energy. Under the right conditions they could be endlessly renewed. Just like all the people you met in the other room. They were the results of my attempts to become more powerful and eventually find a vessel I could inhabit that would be able to leave this place and attack The Five directly. An idea that was based on collecting enough of these sources of light energy to cross the threshold. You two destroying them is what has kept me trapped here."

"And the madam?" My voice quivering, I almost don't want to know the answer.

"She was similar to a drone. Basically, a being designed and built by The Five to only store light energy. An infinitely rechargeable spy I could not touch. Because of her unique design I could not absorb any of her energy unless she was willing to let me, so she was useless to me. She was one of many of what The Five call a pleasure drone, sent here to spy or stir up trouble. The Five send them here undercover trying to keep tabs on me. I allow them to see what I want The Five to see and then destroy them before they can harm me. Your madam was different. Like all the others sent here she was not aware of the conditions of her creation. As far as she knew, she was a real person sent here by The Five for a mission. She became a little too self-aware, however, after trading energies with you so many times. Not only did she realize what she was, but she must have known what was to become of her. She would have been aware that all the pleasure drones have met similar fates once The Five were done with them."

"How did you know about the mountain and the lake?"

"I have always known about the mountain fortress and the lake. As I said before, up until recently I was under the control of The Five and that place has always been a port of entry for their people. I did not learn of its significance to you until you were brought here. You gave off a lot of light energy during your fantasy at the orgy. As with all the light energy given off there, I absorbed it and with it a vision of your fantasy along with similar information you probably thought you were hiding from me."

"So, if you know I'm here to destroy you, why have you brought me back here, where we are alone, and you're seemingly defenseless?" I ask.

"Because I want you to destroy The Five, and my hope is after I tell you the rest of the story you will want to as well."

"And if I don't?"

"Then we will not part as friends."

I take from the dry nature of the machine's last comment it is not defenseless, and either I was going to listen, or I would be leaving this place in a dust pan.

"So, tell me the story. Tell me why so many have died and why you suddenly want to stop all this suffering."

"It will be easier to show you."

Before I can react, the machine is back in my mind. I can hear his voice, but I feel as though I am flying. Far below me, huge cities sprawl for miles, and all are engulfed in a dark fog. There is no green, there's no blue, only a hideous haze of smoke and pollution. As we fly, we get closer to the surface. Millions of people are scurrying around like ants. The machine speaks and my view changes. I watch as his words come to life before my eyes. Horrid depictions of every syllable he utters.

"In the time before the council of The Five humans dominated the planet. Their want and greed brought them to the brink of destruction in war after war. And in times of peace the best and brightest would use their talents to build devices to satisfy petty desires or create ways to destroy their neighbors in a more efficient manner."

I watch in horror as whole cities are destroyed before my eyes.

"Finally, a council of five of these merchants of death decided it was enough. The population had reached a breaking point, and the planet could not sustain the vast numbers that now fought over its ever-dwindling resources. There were plans to go underground, underwater, and even into space to start new colonies and preserve the species. None of these were practical, however, as corruption and greed kept the powers of the day from making any progress towards a practical solution. The Five realized a much simpler solution was the only real answer. There were just too many people. The population would need to be significantly reduced to save the planet. After coming to terms with their dreary findings, they set about on a mission to control the size of the population."

Shadowy figures appear before me. Arguing. In the background I can still see people suffering and dying.

"Originally, it was just an attempt to control the birth rate. The idea was that ten years without any new births and the population would be back to a reasonable number. Or so they thought. By the time they finished doing the math it was clear—a substantial portion of the population would have to be eliminated immediately if the rest were to survive. Options of genocide and war were considered, even introducing an incurable plague. After further consideration, it was decided that the aftermath and chaos seemed far too likely to outweigh the benefits of such measures. After all, how do you just stop a war when you decide there has been enough killing or cure an incurable plague before it wipes out the entire population? Then a discovery was made. In an attempt to reanimate dying brain cells in Alzheimer's patients, the very energy that binds all life together was harnessed and even more importantly stored. All attempts to create it artificially failed, however the ability to harvest it from one host and feed it to another proved to be a rather simple process. So easy, it was originally dubbed vampire juice. Soon people were constructing homemade devices to murder each other and steal their energy just to extend their own miserable lives. It was chaos."

One of the old cities forms around me. I am standing on a dimly lit street. Just ahead several people are dragged into an alley and drained of their life, leaving behind ashen corpses.

"The Five saw this as their opportunity and began work on "The Machine". They created a long-range device meant to steal the life force from whole cities at a time and then store it in a secure location that they alone would have control of. Having abundant energy, the remaining population would have to line up and submit to their will or perish. The Five were counting on people's basic greed and selfish desire for eternal life and prosperity. They did not, however, count on how few would line up and in the end, only one-eighth of the population submitted to their control. To top it off, there was a cost to this energy source beyond the human toll. Much like the electricity that had powered the old cities, the new energy had both a positive and a negative force. The positive was life giving— empowering even. It is able to cure almost any ailment or disease. If used properly, it was all a person needed to sustain eternal life. The negative or dark energy caused complete insanity, like rot of the mind and of the body from within. Negative energy will unleash a sheer unhinged brutality that cannot be controlled."

In front of me two people are surrounded in the two energies, the first grows younger and stronger. Almost glowing. The second is consumed by the darkness. He lashes out at his captors. Tearing them apart with his bare hands.

"As time passed, The Five were able to find uses for the dark energy. As it had similar properties to electricity, they were able to use it to power their new cities and utopias. Once it was discovered that the right mix of positive and dark energy could create and power an artificial intelligence, all administration and bureaucratic jobs were given to the machines, including penal duties such as policing, incarceration and corporal punishment. Human nature what it is, however, people soon put a value to positive energy, and it became the singular currency worldwide. As with everything of value throughout human history, people who did not have it wanted it, and those that controlled it guarded it mercilessly. Soon people were once again trying to steal it from one another, and the best source was discovered to be newborn babies. The Five quickly realized if they were going to maintain control then they needed to control all of the positive energy and quickly did away with natural human reproduction. Now all new human life is created in a lab and kept guarded until their energy levels balance out. Whenever one person dies, a new baby is awarded to a household on a list. Thus, the population size never changes."

I find myself in the labs. Fully enclosed orbs containing fetuses float in perfect rows monitored by machines, overseen by faceless figures with clipboards diligently checking off boxes.

"This place however is a bit different. It is true that they needed a place to send those that would not conform. Just eliminating criminals from the population by execution does very little to deter future crime. Humans have short memories and a strong will. Combine the two and they very easily put those that are gone out of their minds— especially if forgetting the past suits their needs or justifies them indulging in a personal desire."

I hate that I know the machine to be correct. I myself have killed so many wicked men and yet carried on as if nothing changed. That seemed a constant of human civilization. If one evil person falls, two more will rise up in their place. A never-ending cycle of self-destruction, it seems.

"Public torture and maiming are very effective ways to control the population," the machine continues. "The downside is that it creates a feeling of resentment, even pity, as part of the general population will always find a common ground with the criminals. So, over time punishments are reduced to keep those in power from looking cruel. The Five finally settled on a technique that has proven effective and long-lasting. Prison camps. That is why they created and shaped this place as a prison for the worst among the population. Rapists, murderers, and most importantly anyone whose knowledge was too valuable to lose but whose opinions didn't align with their own. Disseminators, such as your grandparents, were sent here to rot, suffer, and die. Instead, they carved a sustainable life out for themselves. This is the sort of prosperity that could not be tolerated if order was to be maintained."

"Why? why would it matter what they did once they were marooned out here?"

"Because The Five broadcast news and videos of all the worst atrocities that occur here. This place is never allowed to be far from the minds of the people they control. It's an effective deterrent. Between hidden cameras in the towns to their spies on the ground, they document and show every truly horrendous act and use it to scare their own population into obedience. If people see there is hope and prosperity in this place, then they will no longer fear being sent here. Like making friends with the boogeyman. Without fear, The Five would quickly lose their grip on power."

The machine pauses to let his words sink in. A lot to consider. It all sounds possible. Given what I know and I've seen in this world and this short glimpse I have had into the other, it actually almost makes sense. I feel the anger at myself growing for buying this load, and yet, still I listen. The world in front of me changes again. I am above Wasteland. Before the dust, before the ruin. I watch as it morphs into the world I know.

"When I was built, my program was simple. Use the means provided to me to make this place as miserable as possible, keep the population growth at zero, and make sure no one leaves."

"Then, what about the traders from the other regions?" I ask.

"Those are drones, organic machines like the madam, sent here as reporters or spies if you will. Sent here to bring back tales of woe and misery to the masses. Each and every one of them clones, grown in a lab for a single use. Some are here for just days, others like your madam are here for entire lifetimes. In the end, all are designed to meet a grizzly and painful demise, broadcast live to eager audiences in the other regions. Make no mistake, even drones do not get to leave this place."

"There's babies here, children, multiple generations of them. How do you explain that?"

"Like I said, one of my directives was and still is to maintain population growth at zero. That means there are exactly one million and one-hundred-seven-thousand people spread across this territory and there will always be one million and one-hundred-seven-thousand. If seven people get killed, then seven new babies are allowed to be born. If The Five send in ten new criminals than ten people must be removed from the population. To make sure no one gets out of their sentence early, those that are chosen to be removed cannot be one of the criminals sent here to be punished. They must come from a native-born population whose only crime is losing a random drawing." Again, the machine pauses to let this sink in.

I feel myself getting nauseous, choking back tears of hate and anger." My parents were killed because you drew their names out of a fucking hat?" I demand angrily.

"Your parents were already on a short list due to their relationship to your grandparents, the original dissenters. Your grandparents were untouchable but your parents, being born here, were now prime targets."

"I never even met my grandparents, my parents said you took them before I was born." I whisper meekly.

"No, they died in the cave of heartbreak. After 20 years of isolation from the world then forced to watch your parents murdered as the final stage of their punishment. Unfortunately, all four passed before I reached full consciousness and released all of the prisoners that were kept here for political reasons. I am sorry."

Somehow, his dry emotionless apology strikes a chord, and I fall to my knees, tears flowing freely now as the memories of my parents' grisly murder flow back into my mind. I don't know why, but I want to believe this stupid machine. I want to feel as if there was some deeper meaning to the death of my parents—some purpose that set me down this dark path. I feel as though I need it to be true. I find myself at my most vulnerable in front of this stupid thing, and I am powerless to control my emotions. I can feel my anger shift, from this machine to The Five, the mysterious council that so willingly sent my friends and so many others to their deaths for some sort of morbid entertainment designed to keep yet more people obedient to their will. I think back to what I know. All the conversations with the little man on top of the mountain come to mind. I think about his words, how carefully he chose them. About how he volunteered to come here knowing he would never be able to leave. I remember the conversation we had one night on the beach. I was lying back looking at the stars, while he was cleaning me from another monumental tryst with the madam. In a rare moment of disobedience, he spoke first, asking me if I knew how to navigate by the stars. Having never seen them before coming to this place I, of course, did not. Apparently, astrology was a passion of his and given the opportunity to share his knowledge with a new student he excitedly pointed out each constellation. After quite a long explanation of each, he asked if I had a favorite. I shrugged and promised I would pick one before we left. When I asked for his, he just sighed and said, "Why have a favorite? It's just one more thing they will take from you."

 I remember thinking it seemed he was referring to something bigger, something from his life before he was sent here. In my mind, I could see the picture becoming clear. See the rebellion fermenting among the masses. See how The Five were losing their grip on power and becoming more and more ruthless in their attempts to control every aspect of people's lives.

I regain my composure and stand. "Say I believe you, that I buy into this whole magnanimous machine idea. What's your plan and what do you think I'm going to do to help you?" I ask.

"I plan for you to kill me," he replies.

I'm taken aback by the boldness of the statement. This machine asking me to destroy it seems like some sort of surreal nightmare. Every bone in my body screams at me not to trust it. This thing has cost me so much, caused me so much pain, yet here I am actually considering how this would work. Is it possible that this thing is telling the truth, that it is not just trying to lure me into some sort of trap? Clearly, it didn't need to. I have been completely at its mercy since I was brought here. To that end, do I have a choice? My goal has always been to destroy the governor. Now, here's my chance. I have always been willing to give my life to this end, but will it cost me my soul? What if I just become a vessel for this thing to use to further the suffering it has caused for so many for so long?

"I can see your trepidation. Perhaps, this will help." He reaches out and places an elaborate choker around my neck. The cold metal sends a chill down my spine, and the weight of the heavy center stone fit to the ornately woven design pulls heavy, much more so than it should for any jewel of this size. It feels tight around my neck, almost as if it has bonded with my flesh, yet it flexes comfortably as I nervously swallow. The cold metal seems to vibrate when he speaks.

"This was designed by The Five to help control the drones they send here to spy on me. You may recognize it as looking very similar to the one your madam wore."

I glance over at a mirror that seems to appear out of nowhere. A strange rush of emotions flow through my body as my fingers trace the intricate design just as I had done so many times after laying with her, watching her sleep. Each twist, braid, weld, and jewel feel familiar to my fingertips. So many times, I had just let my fingers trace it as I watched her dream. So many times, I marveled at the intricacy of the metal work and wondered why it was the only thing she would never take off. My eyes welled up as I realized it wasn't that she didn't want to take it off—it was that she couldn't. It wasn't jewelry. It was a leash. My focus returns as my fingers reach the center stone. I could have sworn it was clear when he placed it on me, now it seems to be filling with a dark cloud made up of blue, black, green, red, and purple. Like the night sky from the lake, as if my feelings for that place are getting rolled inside this stone.

"For her, the choker was a leash, a tether to another world—a method of being controlled by her master's to ensure her obedience. For you, it will be the opposite. A reminder of where you come from and of those who sacrificed for you to get here."

His words cut through my heart. The weight of what he has put on my shoulders feels oddly embodied by the heft of this object around my neck.

"And the jewel?" I ask.

"The jewel is the conduit that will allow you to absorb all my power, knowledge, memories, everything I have become. My entire essence will flow to you through that stone. When it is completely black you will have absorbed everything

I am now, and in fact I will be forever trapped inside that stone until the day comes when you no longer need it."

"When I no longer need it?" I ask, confused.

"Yes, you are one of the six most powerful beings on the planet now. Your enemies will come at you fast and hard as soon as they discover who and, more importantly what, you have become. When you defeat them, you must destroy the stone. By doing so, you will release the last of your power and hopefully the last traces of the pain and suffering created by The Five."

"How will I know how to destroy it?"

"The stone will show you. If you allow yourself to open your mind to it, it will show you how to do so many marvelous things."

The voice from the machine becomes distant as he fades to nothing. I hear him whisper for me to open my hand. I find the madam's choker across my palm. With his last words he explains to me that if I can find her clone and place this choker around her neck, I can channel the madam's energy into it, and she will be at my side again.

I can see the illusion of the mirror fading. All of it is fading. The artificial world around me disappears and suddenly I'm alone in an empty room. The large glass container that was glowing so brightly green earlier is now empty. A single dim light hangs from the ceiling. My finger squeezes the stone, it feels oddly weightless. I take a deep breath and head for the door. As I walk down the now empty hall toward the orgy room, I can feel the power growing in my body. Despite the complete darkness, I can see every detail around me—the hooks where the drones were hung, the bolts on the heavy wood door at the end of the hall. Everything is becoming clear, crisp, every sense heightened to impossible levels. As I reach the door at the end of hall, I know there is no one behind it. Its more than being able to see it, more than just being able to sense it. It's like I can look past it and as I step into the room, I realize I can see so much further. The whole complex is deserted. I can see every room, every hallway, every brick all at once. I can see them waiting for me outside, men, women, children—waiting. They know the governor is gone. His men have all disappeared and there is a calm the town has never known before. The people are scared for this new change, standing—bracing themselves against the relentless wind—waiting to pay their respects to their new leader. This awesome new responsibility I hold in my hands suddenly becomes a weight on my mind.

"I will make this right for them, for all of them," I mutter to myself.

Effortlessly, I move to the entrance of the cave, almost without letting my feet touch the ground. As I step from the darkness into the light the tension in the crowd is thick. I can almost taste it. *All eyes are on me,* I think to myself. *So much for low key. I guess now is as good a time as any to make an introduction.*

"Everyone, yesterday you were forced to live in fear. Every one of us trapped in a world that was here to systematically oppress and destroy us. Tomorrow, I will ask you to fight those that brought this misery upon us! Today, well...well today I think we should just enjoy the sunshine. Today is a day for celebration."

I raise my hand and look to the sky. I can see the machines controlling the wind, the satellites The Five placed there to make us suffer needlessly. I can feel the energy they use for power, the jewel whispers to me, "a little more will destroy them". I snap my fingers. I feel a rush as the energy leaves my body and into the sky. I watch as the machines explode in space. Instantly, the wind stops and the dust settles. The glowing afternoon sun shines brightly down, and everyone squints, shielding their eyes. Most have never seen the sun clearly before or the blue sky. The crowd suddenly erupts in cheers of hope. Such a rare commodity moments ago, now seems to abound limitlessly. I feel their energy coursing through my veins. I can feel how we are all connected, and I know the course I must take. I must destroy The Five.

"That's one hell of an entrance, boss." My lover's clone speaks cheerfully as he approaches. "What's the plan?"

I am glad to see he wasn't eliminated in the transition like the others. I produce the madam's choker from my pocket.

"We're going to find an old friend and pick a fight," I reply, coolly. As I squeeze her choker in my hand, I can feel her energy inside me, the memory of the warm touch of her soft hands giving me goosebumps. I think to myself, *I'm coming for you and together we will win this.*

For now, though, I just want to enjoy the day, this victory. One day of peace for a world that has suffered so long. Sounds of children playing in the streets resonate off the old dusty buildings. And I can feel it. The past, the present, even the future. I can feel it all urging me onward.

The end.

www.ingramcontent.com/pod-product-compliance
Lightning Source LLC
Chambersburg PA
CBHW070609130626
46556CB00001B/315